GETTING IT

Twisted

ALLY AVERY

Contents

Author's Note

CONTENT WARNINGS (CONTAINS SPOILERS)

This story contains subject matters some readers might find upsetting, such as discussion and/or imagery of depression and mental health struggles, mentions of suicide and suicidal ideation, self-harm and self-destructive behavior, mentions of past sexual assault/rape, coercion into sexual intercourse without protection, pain or injury during sex, homophobic slurs, mentions of drug use (voluntary and involuntary), drug overdose of a secondary character, death of a family member, codependency and/or inappropriate/toxic attachment, mentions of child abuse, neglect, and child sexual abuse.

Please keep these potential triggers in mind and prioritize your mental health.

Playlist

Numb To The Feeling — Chase Atlantic

Bad Kids — Black Lips

He's a Rebel — The Crystals

Nancy Boy — Placebo

more than friends — Isabel LaRosa

Animal Nitrate — Suede

Strange Birds — Birdy

Let It Go — Chandler Leighton, LØ Spirit

when the party's over — Billie Eilish

Sorry — Halsey

Heavy — Citizen Soldier, SkyDxddy

Full Spotify playlist can be found on my website allyaveryauthor.com.

Chapter 1

NATHAN

I'VE HAD SEX WITH men who hated me. Or rather, men who hated their attraction to me.

I've had sex with men who craved more from me than I could give them.

This one falls somewhere in between: a six-foot-tall "straight" guy I picked up outside a bar, jacked up like a quarterback, who speaks in grunts and kisses me with a desperate fervor as he pushes me up against the motel room wall.

He's a good kisser, and he takes my hand and presses it to the bulge in his jeans. Fine. This is easy. He'll give me what I want, and then I'll be on my way.

Before long, I have him on the bed with his thighs spread wide. I kneel in front of him and unbuckle his jeans, and my mouth is inches from his cock when my phone rings.

"Hold on." I slick my palm with spit and stroke him while I fetch my phone with my free hand. I'm not sure why I answer the call; I suppose part of me wants to fuck with the dude in more ways than one.

I'm silent during most of the conversation, replying yes and no and "I understand" where appropriate while I keep stroking the dude's cock.

His gaze is fiery on mine, brows knitted, jaw worked tight. He looks furious, but I've seen that look before; he's just impatient and horny.

When the call's done, I feel cold, and my vision blurs. I figure it's the booze, or the lack of a proper dinner. Whatever.

"What was that about?" the dude asks.

I chuck the phone away and take him into my mouth to shut him up. Big-cocked motherfucker as he is, I have to fight to do it: stretch my jaw real wide and relax my throat to take him all the way inside. He groans and grabs onto my hair. I start sucking him proper, but it's like something's itching at the back of my skull, and it's not his hand. It's different, it's—

I pull back. The grip on my hair tightens.

"Hey," says the dude. His fingers tangle into my locks and stroke my scalp, almost gently. "What was that call about?"

"None of your business."

"It *is* my business, if it's got you all upset."

"Who's upset?" I snap. "Look, you want your dick sucked or not?"

He raises an eyebrow at me, likely more for my tone than my words. "You're not so sweet now, are you?"

"Never said I was sweet." I try to get off the bed, but the dude grabs my arm.

"Is sex off the table now?" He looks disappointed, though it's not a puppy-eyed disappointment; he's ... annoyed. I can work with that.

"No. Take off your shirt."

The dude smiles. "Bossy. I like it."

He wrestles out of his tight shirt and helps me with my own, then my belt. I feel his gaze on me as I fish a packet of lube and a condom out of my pocket.

"Damn." His hand runs up my waist, thumb sliding over a nipple. "You're beautiful." His other hand unzips my fly, and now I'm at least halfway hard again—good.

I lie on my back and yank my jeans off. I hand him the condom while I tear open the lube packet with my teeth and get my fingers to my hole. All the while, he watches me. His enraptured gaze slides across my face, my body, down to where I'm hard and wanting and working myself open with lube-slick fingers.

I muster up a smirk. "Enjoying the view?"

His rough hands stroke my thighs, pushing them apart to spread me wide. "You never told me your name."

"Will knowing my name help you fuck me better?"

He scoffs, the spell broken, and positions himself between my legs. "You ready?"

I grit my teeth. Why ask? "Just do it."

The truth sinks in at the same time as his cock. Once it does, the meaning erupts and whirls in my mind alongside the initial burn, and his hands on me, his cock in me, his thumb digging into my hip bone ...

"My mother is dead."

"What?" he grunts, red-faced and heavy on top of me. The shitty motel bed creaks with the thrusts of his hips.

"It's what you wanted to know, right? What the phone call was about." I hike my knees up high, urging him to go deeper and to reach a spot that sharpens the softness in me. "They called to break the news—she's dead."

"Shit." He slows down his thrusts. "Was she sick or somethin'?"

"You could say that." A flash of memories hits me—a screeching voice and a door slamming shut—but I push them away as quick as they came. "Did I tell you to stop?"

The dude snorts and slams into me hard, smirking as a moan escapes me. "You're real mouthy for someone whose mom just died."

"Shut me up, then." I grab his wrist and put his hand to my throat.

A hiss between clenched teeth. "You're so fucked up."

I glare at him through my bangs. As if I didn't know that already. Guys usually don't care about my crossed wires when they're coming down my throat or stuffing my ass with their cocks. Not that I give a shit about what they think. As long as they give me what I want, it's all good. And as long as they don't try to cuddle me afterward. Hate it when guys who look like they could choke me out in a headlock want to treat me like some princess after they've shot their load.

The guy finally gets the memo. He flips me over, and his rough, callused hand hooks around my throat as he starts plowing into me like he's trying to prove a point.

Yeah, that's right. This is what I need, this is what I need ...

Let the pleasure wash through me, together with the pain. Let it take me away from this dank motel room to a place where reality doesn't hit quite as hard.

"You like this big dick, bitch?"

I give a muffled groan in reply.

"Twinks like you usually squeal like pigs when I fuck 'em." He lets go of my throat and twists his fingers into my hair, shoving my face into the mattress. The new angle makes him hit my prostate, and I can no longer hold in my moans.

"I'm gonna make you fucking come." He pushes me down until I lie prone, my cock leaking and rubbing onto the sheets.

Oh god, he's right. I feel it building, winding into a knot of tension in my groin. He bites the shell of my ear. Twists my nipple so hard I cry out. My ass clenches around him as my mind blanks, my toes curl, my vision blurs.

He grunts like an animal when he comes too, right after me. The weight of his body lands on the bed. Then he snaps off the condom, and his huge, heavy arm wraps around me, pulling me close.

My head spins. Nausea rises up my throat. The usual postorgasmic bliss turns to dread as reality comes crashing back down.

My mother is gone, but that's not the issue.

The issue is I now have a reason to return to Springvale, and knowing myself, I won't be able to resist seeking out Daniel once I'm there.

Chapter 2

DANIEL

THE PARTY SWARMS ALL around me. I'm one with the music, moving to the sound of that wicked beat ...

A look to the side sends my head spinning from one too many sips from the keg. The spot next to me is empty. Where the hell is Nathan? He was here a minute ago. Or maybe ten minutes ago. He should be here and celebrate with me.

My unsteady legs lead me to the hallway. From the furthest door comes a loud thud and a muffled voice I don't recognize.

"Get him on the bed."

Then a voice I'd know anywhere, from any distance, in any plane of time.

Nathan. He groans, but it's not a groan of pleasure. Not at all.

Laughter, and a third voice. "That's it. Keep him like that."

What the hell?

My chest rises with a shaky breath. In and out. I close my hand around the doorknob and turn ...

"Hello? Earth to Daniel." Lydia's fingers snap in front of my face. "You could at least kiss me back, you know. I'm trying here."

I drag a hand over my face, trying to wipe off the remnants of the daydream. I haven't thought about that night in a long time. What the hell set it off? Even after five years, the memory is so easily summoned.

"Sorry," I say. "Work wrung me out."

"Yeah, I can see that." Her ass presses into my groin as she straddles me on the bed and peels back the zipper of my work uniform. "Let me help you feel better, baby."

I consider letting her do it—focusing on her hands trailing down my body and stroking my thighs, because what guy in his right mind would turn down a blow job? But it's no use. My dick is soft with disinterest, and I'm not in the mood to steer my thoughts to where it'll go hard.

It becomes clear to me then: it's not just the in-this-moment sex I don't want.

It's her. It's *us*.

Lydia's nice enough, she's pretty enough, and when she smiles, her eyes twinkle in a way that makes me think of soap bubbles in the open summer sky. But there's nothing in me that burns for her. There's lust but only the automatic reactions of my body. There's no longing when she's not around. There's no love, no hate, no happy, no sad. Nothing. I'm coursed through with numbness, all the way to my core. I know what could thaw me, but *he* is a thousand miles away, or dead for all I know.

Lydia, who must feel my stiffness everywhere except for where it should be, glances up. "Something wrong?"

"Yeah," I say. "This isn't working."

"Oh. Well, tell me what you want me to do, then. What'll make you feel good."

"No, Lydia." I push her gently off me and slide off the bed. "*This.*" I point between me and her. "It's not gonna work."

Her frown deepens. "What do you mean?"

Am I gonna have to spell it out to her? We've been together for, what, two months? Long enough for her to notice how my eyes glaze over when she tells me about her pet chinchilla and tarot readings and the news. Long enough for her to notice my unenthusiastic hugs when I greet her after work.

"You're breaking up with me?" She straightens her blouse and bounces off the bed. Her accusatory glare is a relief, strangely enough. Out of anger or sadness, I prefer the former.

"You can still come here and hang out at parties," I offer half-heart-edly. "Tonight, for example, we—"

"No, thanks," she snaps. "I don't wanna hang out with your *room-mates*, Daniel."

Something in the way she says it makes my hackles rise, and I no longer care about letting her down or being hospitable—not if she's gonna make snide comments about my friends. She's in my bedroom, in my house, and I want her gone.

"Suit yourself." I turn my back on her and start rearranging the pile of books on my windowsill, hoping she'll get the message.

"You're not the nice guy everyone thinks you are, you know."

"No?" I say in a dull voice, suspecting where this conversation is going. Might as well humor her; I owe her that much. "What am I, then?"

"You act like you're so mysterious, with your drawings and your brooding eyes. Guess what, you're just an asshole who thinks you're better than everyone else!"

Brooding? I cross my arms and face her. "All right. So I'm not nice, I'm an asshole and all-around uncool. Anything else, or are you done?"

"No, I'm not done." She balls her hands into fists at her sides, and for a moment, she looks like she wants to hit me. "How about you make something of your life and go to college like the rest of us? Or are you planning to be a janitor for the rest of your life?"

Maintenance technician. Not janitor. But what's the use in correcting her if it won't be enough to make her leave? What would Nathan say? *Fuck off, I'm bored of you now, leave?*

But I'm not like him, and there's no use in wishing I was.

"I'm sorry," I say, and I am.

I could've dragged our relationship on forever, and despite what insults she's hurled at me now, I'm pretty sure she would've let me. I suppose that's the problem; I'm cursed to forever pine for what I can't have and be bored to tears once I have it in my hands. Unless it's *him*. But it's never going to be him.

Getting the message at last, Lydia yanks the door open and turns around to send me a final, seething glare.

"You know what, Daniel? Fuck you. You don't deserve me anyway."

"Bye, Lydia."

If Nathan taught me anything, it's to always get the last word.

The front door slams shut, shaking the walls of the entire house. I wait until I hear the rumble of Lydia's car before I make my way downstairs. As expected, George—my cousin and roommate—is there waiting for me.

"What the fuck was that about?"

"What?" I make a beeline for the kitchen, intent on a quick dinner to wolf down.

"What do you think?" George says, following behind me. "Lydia! I've never seen her that pissed off. What the fuck did you do?"

There's nothing of note in the fridge other than April's almond milk, George's protein shakes, and days-old takeout pizza I don't dare to touch. I give up and face George.

"Things weren't working." Better be vague and let him think I just need a little encouragement and not—

"*What* wasn't working? You're never going to find something long-lasting if you don't look into these things, you know. Reflect and all that."

Oh yeah? As if you know so much about it? I want to quip at him, but then again, I suppose he does know a thing or two about relationships. He and April must've been together for over a year now, and I still have trouble wrapping my head around how those two make it work.

"I didn't feel anything when I looked at her or thought about her, all right?" I say with a shrug. "Wasn't her fault. Just wasn't right."

"And what would it take to make it right?"

His tone is too patronizing, too "I know best, little cousin," too ... worried. All it does is make me want to worry him some more, in some stupid surge of rebellion.

"You want to know why it didn't work out between me and Lydia? She wasn't *him*. Is that what you want me to say?"

He squints, staring at me as if he can't be quite sure he heard right. "What did you just say?"

I clench my jaw and try to ignore the creeping sense of regret for what I just said. But George doesn't do well with being ignored.

"Hey! What the hell did you mean by that?"

I shrug again, mouth a thin, tense line.

"Daniel, don't you dare. Don't tell me you're still thinking about *him*. Seriously?" He throws his hands in the air, the vein in his temple already red and bulging. "Have you forgotten how he treated you?"

"No." I haven't forgotten. And I don't want to.

"Look." George puts his hands on my shoulders. I fight the urge to shake them off. "You don't need to figure out what went wrong with Lydia just yet. April's biology class is coming to the party tonight. Maybe you can find someone there—a rebound or whatever."

Find someone else who'll disappoint me so I can disappoint them in return? No, thanks. My sullen expression seems enough to convey my line of thought, because George sighs and lets go of me.

"On the subject of … *Nathan*"—he says the last word carefully, jaw tight, as if the name itself pisses him off—"did you hear about his mom?"

"What about her?"

"She's dead. She was found in her house. Overdose, probably. Choked on her own vomit."

My stomach turns over, and images start flashing across my mind. The first time I saw Nathan's mom, she sat on the front porch, smoking a cigarette. Her long dark hair glistened in the sun, her slender limbs exposed in a tight black dress. I remember my twelve-year-old self thinking, *Wow, she looks like a movie star.* Nathan hopped off the back of my bike, and she stormed over to us and snatched his upper arm. Nails digging into his flesh, she dragged him toward the house while he glared daggers at her.

Theresa Antler, beautiful but terrible. I imagine her now cold and pale, lips blue, on the floor of Nathan's childhood home.

"When?"

"About a week ago. Dad called me on Monday."

"A week ago? What the hell?"

George shrugs. "I've been busy. Family law classes started this week. I'm telling you now, aren't I?" Now that he mentions it, he looks exhausted, his brown hair more ruffled than styled, and his usual sun-kissed complexion is chalky and pale.

"What about her house?" I ask.

"What about it?"

"She had no husband and no other children. It's gonna go to *him*. Isn't it?" Realization strikes, and my eyes go wide. "George, you don't think he'll ... "

"Do I think he'll come here to sort out the house?" George clicks his tongue. "I dunno. Not that it's much of a house anyway. Might as well level it to the ground and sell off the land. Besides, why go through the effort when he could get it done with a few phone calls?" George looks at me, *really* looks at me, and his face twists into a strange expression. "Unless ..."

"Unless what?"

He scowls and looks away. "Never mind."

I clench my jaw, trying hard to shut the floodgates of memories that threaten to resurface. If I'm not careful, they'll be as clear in my mind as the day they happened. For all I don't want to forget the good moments we shared, the bad ones are enough to make me damn near catatonic.

A twinkle in vivid green eyes. A mocking tilt to perfect lips. *What did you think—that we're some lovey-dovey couple now? Fucking is just fucking.*

All I want now is to vegetate for a few hours before the party starts. Maybe continue the work on my latest drawing to keep my mind off the things I've learned.

"By the way," George says. "Weren't you supposed to have dinner at Gillian's tonight?"

"Oh, right. Shit." After Lydia and the breakup, the dinner with my mom totally slipped my mind.

The thing with her is it's never just dinner. The question is what she *really* wants.

"Danio!" My sister stretches her arms toward me in her wheelchair, smiling the brightest of smiles.

"How are you, sis?" I embrace her thin shoulders and stroke her pale cheek. At least *she's* happy to see me. My mom, on the other hand ...

"I see you finally decided to show up," she says and nods to the table, hair bunched into a tight knot. "Dinner's getting cold."

I gesture toward Jessie. "Let me help her."

"No. Sit down and eat."

I do as she says to shut her up. Jessie smiles at me from the edge of the table as Gillian feeds her small spoonfuls of chili.

"I wasn't aware your job worked you late," Mom says.

"It didn't." I won't tell her dinner slipped my mind, but I don't feel like lying either.

"Still no plans to return to college, I presume?"

I roll my eyes. First Lydia, and now my mom too? "At least I've got a job now, haven't I?"

Compared to the year I could barely get out of bed, I'm doing well. Better, at least. My job at Springvale Community Center gets me working with my hands, keeps me fit and on my feet. The pay is abysmal, and though I don't want to be stuck doing it forever, it's fine for now. At least until I feel well enough to start studying again. My days of dreaming of an ambitious career were numbered to begin with, but my attempts at starting college right after high school ... Well, they went down the drain, to say the least.

Gillian averts her eyes from her daughter, and for once, she looks at me. Unlike George, who takes after my uncle and father in appearance,

I take after my mother. We have the same dirty-blond hair, blue eyes, and square jaw. By this time of year, the skin around our noses and cheeks is dotted with freckles from the summer sun.

But that's where our similarities end. Gillian's hair is graying around her temples, and she looks perpetually stressed—almost ill. Frown lines are etched deep between her brows, as has been the case ever since the divorce. Or now that I think about it, ever since Jessie's dramatic birth.

"I just thought you'd make something of yourself," Mom says, "now that you don't have that awful boy nipping at your heels anymore."

I choke on a mouthful of food. *That awful boy ...*

"Danio," Jessie says, fighting to get her words out. "Wh-Who does she mean?"

I force the food down my throat and swallow thickly. "Nathan. She means Nathan." Because curse the day my mother would ever take his name into her mouth. My dad was even worse. I've never seen him so angry as when he found out Nathan was gay. God forbid his son would have a faggot for a best friend.

Jessie giggles. "But Nathan isn't awful."

"At least you cut your hair." Gillian nods at my hairstyle: a short undercut with a messy, longer part at the top. It isn't new though. I cut my signature shoulder-length hair off when I left college four years ago. "Did you hear about his mother?"

"Yes." I stare gloomily into my plate, hoping she'll drop the subject.

"It was just as well if you ask me. Bad seeds the lot of them, those Antlers. Her father used to lurk around downtown, clearly drunk or high off his mind. Did you know?"

"Mom," I say, clenching my hand around my barely used spoon. "Why did you invite me again?"

She pins me with a cold look. "Don't be smart with me, Daniel."

"I'm not. Remember?" My sarcastic smile makes her mouth purse as if she's eaten something sour, and she turns her attention back to my sister.

"I'm remaking your old bedroom into a rehab room for Jessie. This is your chance to retrieve any items you might miss. Most of it is junk, of course."

"Of course," I say between gritted teeth. Never mind that I might not be in the mood to revisit my old room, but explaining why would only invite my mother to bring up my past again.

And so, after dinner, I walk down the corridor to my room.

Not much remains of the state I left it in two years ago. My bed, desk, and art supplies are all transferred to my new bedroom in the two-story house George inherited from his grandmother.

What remains is the bookcase I neglected to bring and the stuff in the closet I haven't laid eyes on in years. The very thought of opening that box of worms has my heart pumping harder in my chest.

Most of the shelves are filled with artwork I drew when I was young. Animals. People. The view outside my window. But there's other stuff too, like a coal pencil sketch depicting two boys holding hands, standing on top of a hill that overlooks the city.

Under the sketch is a plastic folder of Polaroids. An invisible hand squeezes my heart at the sight.

The first photo is of the two of us. Nathan makes an exaggerated grimace for the camera and holds up two fingers in the peace sign, arm slung over my shoulders. Nathan with his studded belt, dyed hair, and silver earrings, and me with my long dirty-blond hair and baggy T-shirt. Another photo is of me alone, perhaps from the same occasion. My eyes are half-lidded and dazed as I exhale a cloud of smoke from the joint in my hand.

Then come the class photos. Why my mom made sure to save them I can only guess at. Perhaps she still had faith in me back in middle school.

The fifth-grade child version of myself glares impassively at the camera, mouth downturned in a frown. I look so depressed it's almost funny. Experiencing it, however? That was far from fun. Dark thoughts of harming myself came almost daily, and I was invisible even to my parents. Especially to my parents.

The difference between my fifth- and sixth-grade photos is so striking I have to do a double take. From one year to the next, my eyes are noticeably brighter, the corners of my mouth upturned in a smile. It's as if the hard dark shell of me has cracked. What happened between those two years to cause a change so fundamental?

Nathan. Nathan happened.

Two months into the fall semester of sixth grade, a new boy waltzed into the classroom. Backpack askew over one shoulder, he had a toothpick in his mouth and a messy mop of dark curls for hair. He looked utterly bored, lacking the nerves you'd expect from a transfer student. There was a thin-boned sharpness to him, and a jaded look in his eyes that the rest of us lacked. It made him seem older than his age. Mature in an unsettling sort of way. A twelve-year-old kid was not supposed to have seen as much as he had.

His gaze swept over the classroom and landed on me. I might have imagined the way his eyebrows lifted or the minute twist to the corner of his mouth. Or maybe he knew, even then, that all it would take was for him to sit next to me during recess and ask, "What's that you're drawing?," and we'd be joined at the hip for the following six years.

Even in the school photos, his striking features and boyish charm are plain to see. Not that I noticed at that age how stunning he was—at least not in that way. But other people's reactions to him were impossible to miss.

How he placated the teachers when he hadn't done his assignments on time. Or how he blamed one of the school's bullies for pulling the fire alarm during math class when the culprits were none other than me and him. His ease in charming people when he had the mind for it. When he *didn't* have the mind for it, well … Let's just say his looks couldn't help him with everything.

He was a dick to everyone else but not to me, and that was dangerous for a kid who'd never had anyone pay him the time of day.

I was too shy and bookish to make other friends. George tried to take me under his wing, but his one-year-older jock buddies found me weird and withdrawn.

Nathan did what George could not. Nathan in turn had his own peculiarities, and we fit together like two jagged, leftover puzzle pieces. Him outgoing and reckless and endlessly bored. Me with a head full of ideas and a rebellious fire in my heart that Nathan happily stoked. Before long, we were burning in it, and that fire lasted for six whole years.

And then … poof. He was gone, and there was a time when I felt like nothing would ever fill the void he left behind.

I grit my teeth and dump the photos back into the box. I should let my mom throw them out. I definitely shouldn't bring them with me.

But that's exactly what I do.

The moment I step inside the hallway back home, George pushes a tequila shot into my hand. Judging by his flushed skin and his goofy smile, he's already drunk.

Music and voices merge into one pulsating, headache-inducing force. It jacks up my heart rate, makes me sweat. But it beats being alone. When you're trying to keep your mind off somebody, loneliness is the real killer.

At some point, April joins me by the awkward spot between the stairs, the kitchen, and the living room. Her wild mane of long black hair drapes over my shoulder as she leans to speak into my ear.

"I'm glad this many people showed up. The weather's gone insane."

It's not an exaggeration. Outside the windows, the rain is absolutely pouring down, and thunder rumbles in the distance. September is a little late for thunderstorms in Oregon, even after the unusually hot summer we've had.

I turn to April. "Any potential roommates to vet?" Our last roommate moved out a month ago after George kicked him out for hiding hard drugs in his room.

"George takes care of that stuff," April says with a dismissive wave. "But I've already told him we could use the spare room for a pet instead. Maybe a guinea pig." Her tattooed fingers grab my upper arm. "I heard about Lydia, by the way."

"George told you? Great." I take another sip of beer, already drunker than I should be at this hour.

"Don't worry. You'll find someone new."

"Yeah, sure." But that someone won't be him. And I shouldn't wish it was him. I shouldn't even think about him. Hating him annoys me, but missing him makes me hate myself.

April winks at me and sips her obscenely colorful drink through a straw. "Just say the word, and I'll fix you up with someone. How about Hailey?" She nods at a brunette in high heels. "Her boyfriend broke up with her two weeks ago." She grabs my hand. "Come on, I'll introduce you guys."

She starts dragging me into the living room, but for some reason, the thought of talking with someone new makes my skin crawl.

"Maybe later."

"Like I said, just say the word." She winks again and elbows me in the side.

Sometimes—like right now—I feel like April and George act less like friends and more like some kind of parental figures, which is odd, considering they're only one year my senior. But maybe I need it. God knows my real parents never paid much attention to me. Sometimes I feel like they've forgotten they even have a son. My dad has a new life with his new family in Portland, while my mom has spent the last fifteen years ignoring me in favor of her daughter.

As for April and George, however, the line between helpful and patronizing is thin, especially when I feel like I'm barely hanging on.

I take in the crowd again and spot the girl April mentioned, Hailey. She helps herself to a refill from the keg, meets my gaze, and smiles before she scurries off to rejoin her friends. She's cute, I guess. But cute is not enough to sway me.

One-night stands bring me little satisfaction, although I've had them, and I do them. But it's like scratching an itch that comes back tenfold a few days afterward. There's no real point to it except to temporarily quell my loneliness, but even for that, it's rarely helpful.

Maybe I should lay off sex for a while until I find someone I actually give a fuck about. Maybe I should crawl into a cave until I'm touch-starved enough to properly function. Or slither into a hole, change skin like a snake, and rise from the undergrowth ... A new me, without a five-year-old hole in my heart.

Maybe I should forget about girls and look for a guy instead. The thing is every time I've tried has been a disaster.

It goes like this: They either remind me too much of Nathan, and I get all bogged down in old memories and emotions. Or they're too unlike him and my attraction fizzles out like a doused match.

They can't be too ... *nice*. Which sounds fucking weird when I think about it, but it's true. There's no reason to push them into the mattress if they don't talk back and annoy me. With girls, I don't need that angry switch to flip, but with guys it's different. And I always found myself the most turned on by Nathan when he annoyed the shit out of me. Maybe he's caused some permanent damage in my brain and made me unable to fuck any guy who isn't him.

I bet he'd like that.

I clench my teeth. Damn it all. One more beer, then I'll go talk to Hailey. I might never find someone I'm special to and who's special to me, but at least I can drown my sorrows in booze and sex.

As I look for a beer opener, I catch a glimpse in the kitchen window.

A car down by the road. A red car. A red Ford Mustang, with a spray-painted black hood.

No way. It can't be ... can it? Either I'm drunker than I thought, or the rain's playing tricks on me.

"Hey, where are you going?" George slurs in the hallway as I put my sneakers on. "The sky's falling out there."

A bolt of lightning strikes as soon as I get outside the front door, followed by a loud crack of thunder. I take shelter under the patio roof and peer into the rain-soaked darkness.

When we were sixteen, Nathan and I stumbled upon an old car in the middle of the forest. It was covered in branches and debris but not beyond saving. We set to work, educating ourselves in car mechanics and obtaining spare parts.

We were supposed to go on a cross-country road trip after high school. The car would be our escape car, we said. But when push came to shove, Nathan went on his own and left me behind. I haven't seen that car for over five years. It's almost surreal to see it here now.

I sway drunkenly on my feet, grabbing onto a support beam. Damp wooden splinters dig into my palm, and the hair at the back of my neck stands up.

"Looking for something?"

That voice…

I spin around. The world tilts on its axis, all misaligned and disjointed. A cloud of cigarette smoke dissolves, revealing green eyes, black hair, and the tilt of a perfect mouth.

No. No way…

The music and chatter from the party inside fade to a buzz in my ears, as does the rain. All I see and hear is *him*.

Nathan.

And five years of heartbreak and sorrowful anger rushes back to me all at once, as fresh and raw as when it first happened.

I dash forward and seize the collar of his leather jacket. There's a dull thud as his back hits the wall, and the cigarette he was smoking drops from his mouth.

"What the fuck are you doing here?" I growl.

His vivid green eyes glitter, his strong dark eyebrows contrasting his otherwise androgynous features. "I could ask you the same."

His voice. That damn smooth drawl. I once told myself I'd forgotten his way of speaking, but I know now that wasn't even remotely true. I'm stunned enough that I don't even question what the hell he means. *I could ask you the same.* Why? What?

"Tell me," I grit out. "What. Are. You. Doing here?"

"Didn't hear the news? Dear Mother Theresa got herself shot up with enough dope to finally kill her. I'm here to sort out her shit."

"That doesn't explain why you're here on my front porch."

He shrugs. "Maybe I wanted to see you."

"So you thought you'd just hang out here and look through windows like a fucking creep? How did you even know I live here?"

I shove him one more time, hard against the wall, and this time, it gets a frown out of him and a buzz of satisfaction from me.

"What can I say, I just wanted to do some recon," he says, and the corner of his lips curls into a smile. That damn smile ... It's the smile of someone who knows the secrets of the world—the smile of someone who knows us mortals will never understand what it's like to have his good looks and unerring confidence.

The air crackles between us with another strike of lightning, followed by a rupture of thunder so loud I feel like my eardrums are gonna burst. At the same time, the front door opens wide.

"Yo, Danny," George slurs, relying on the door handle to support his weight. "What the fuck are you doing out here?"

A jolt of anxiety goes through me at the thought of him finding out what exactly I'm doing here—and with who—but when I look back to the space where Nathan just stood, it's empty.

He's gone. The fuck? How did he get away so fast?

George points to the still-burning cigarette by my feet. "I thought you'd quit?"

"I have." I stomp it out and make for the door. "Come on."

As soon as we get back to the lively chaos of drunken, happy people, what happened outside feels like some kind of fever dream.

Just to make sure, I look out the window. The rain is easing up, and the red Ford Mustang is gone, leaving nothing but a trail of wet leaves in its wake.

Chapter 3

NATHAN

I CLIMB INTO THE driver's seat, completely soaked through and shivering. A glance into the rearview mirror tells me I look a mess, with clumps of hair plastered to my forehead and a haunted gleam to my eyes.

It's this fucking town. It puts me on edge.

So does Daniel.

It wasn't supposed to happen like this. Tonight I was supposed to be a wallflower gazing into his life, but then he had to come and pluck me off the wall—or more like, shove me *into* the wall.

I should have left him alone for now. I should have gone to see him another day. But no, my first order of business when I came back to town after a ten-hour drive was to look up the address of my former best friend and go ogle at him through the window like a fucking stalker.

He was so pissed off when he saw me. Furious. Has living with George and his anger issues rubbed off on him, or did me leaving really affect him that much?

It was so long ago though. A different time. A different life. And we used to be friends. Does that mean nothing to him?

Fuck, I'm too tired for this shit.

As I swerve out on the street, I can't stop thinking about how he looked inside that house, among all those happy, drunken people. Unlike them, he seemed so ... dejected. Shoulders slumped, head bent down, gaze dead and numb. He used to get like that sometimes when he got too into his head. Maybe now that he doesn't have me to lighten his mood, he's completely taken over by it—the gloominess.

Gloomy doesn't even begin to describe how he was when he pushed me up against that wall. Goddamn. I liked seeing him like that though. All pissed off and intense, with those thick muscled arms bearing down on me. He's no longer the skinny, long-limbed teenager I remember.

He's a man now.

Those baby-blue eyes are the same, as are his long lashes and freckles. But his jaw has sharpened, the last bit of baby fat gone from his face, and the way he looked at me ... The very thought makes the crotch of my jeans feel tight. I sure wouldn't mind getting those hands on me again.

The rainfall slows to a trickle as I turn into the downtown district of Springvale. Everything's closed at this hour except for the odd gas station and a handful of bars. Other than the surrounding nature—if you care about that sort of thing—this town's only saving grace is its proximity to a fairly reputable college. At this time of year, the area is flooded with students.

I pass the sign for Springvale University and turn left in the three-way crossing by the edge of the city center. Dark groves of trees line up on either side as I come onto Wayward Road. The streetlights grow sparser and sparser and die some ten miles on.

Around the next curve of the road, there it is: a lonely gray wooden house, tucked into a burrow of trees. I stop the car and rip the key out of the ignition.

Silence.

Dead silence.

Why did I come here again? I mean, I know why, but damn ... My skin starts to tingle from a mere glance at that house, and I have to do a whole lot more than glance at it.

A dog barks somewhere down the road. There's a movement in the rearview mirror as my old neighbor, Ennis, comes limping toward me with his cane. His German shepherd zips past my car like a dark shadow and paces the front of the house, whining and barking like mad.

"Jagger!" Ennis yells. "Come back here, girl." His shrill whistle tears through the air.

I climb out of the car and fish a cigarette out of my pocket.

Ennis's watery gray eyes fix on me. "What are you doing here, boy?"

I keep the cigarette in my mouth unlit, hands in my pockets. "Didn't you hear? My mama went and croaked."

"I know," Ennis says. "Wayne Hastings himself came a-knocking."

"Oh yeah?" I light the cigarette and ask the one thing they didn't tell me on the phone call. "Where'd they find her? In what room?"

"Why don't you ask at the station?" Ennis grumbles. "Unless you have a spare key, you oughta pay them a visit regardless."

"Why would I have a spare?" When I left this place, I had no plans of coming back.

"Good luck getting inside that door, then, boy. It's locked. The cops have the key."

I grit my teeth. I know damn well the cops have the key. "I'll manage."

The dog—Jagger—has stopped barking, but she's still pacing the yard, letting out wary little whines now and again. Ennis and I gaze toward the house looming in the darkness.

"I'm almost blind, boy," Ennis says slowly, "but not so blind that I didn't understand what was going on here."

My voice comes out bitter around a cloud of smoke. "Oh yeah? Why didn't you do anything, if you knew so much?"

"I don't stick my nose into other people's business."

"Then what's this you're doing now?"

Ennis studies me, forehead creasing into deep dark grooves. "You shouldn't be back here, boy."

"I'm not. I'm just gonna fix up the place and sell it."

"Are you, now?"

"Someone's bound to buy it. Why else would I be here?"

"Well, get it done, then, boy, as soon as you can. Don't linger around here."

"Is that a threat?" My sarcastic tone and accompanying grin don't seem to work on old Ennis. He stares at me blankly before pursing his lips and giving another whistle.

"Come here, girl!" This time, Jagger obeys, and they continue down the road.

"Yeah, go ahead, don't let me keep you. Crazy old man," I mutter under my breath.

As I turn back to the house, an unease that wasn't there before courses through me. And suddenly I wish Jagger and Ennis would've stayed a little while longer.

I open the trunk of my car and rip out the tattered gym bag containing most of the stuff I own. Then I start trudging up the overgrown path toward the house. My house.

The house I was born in. The house I grew up in. The twisted times, the lonely times. The horror my mother put me through.

Darkness presses further in on my vision the closer I get. The house is little more than a shack, with rough wood-panel walls bleached gray from the sun and many years of neglect. The stairs creak as I walk up the patio and try the door. Locked, like Ennis said it would be. If the door were as run-down as the rest of the house, I could've kicked it in. But this door is a remnant of my grandfather, reinforced with a lock on either side; I need the key to unlock it even from within.

No matter. I go around the back. I have to watch where I'm going; there's so much shit lying around on the lawn—wires, old car wheels, dingy furniture—all half-hidden by knee-high weeds and grass.

I imagine myself dousing the house in gasoline and lighting a match. I'd turn my back on the fire while flames licked into the open black sky.

What I do instead is grab a decent-sized rock from the ground and chuck it as hard as I can into the hallway window.

The sound of shattering glass is deafening in the silence and fills me with a strange sense of satisfaction. Using an old chopping block as a stepping stone, I heave myself up, taking care not to cut myself as I crawl inside.

I land on the wooden floor, glass crunching under my feet. I flick the light switch in the hallway, but nothing happens. Electricity's shut off? Oh well, I could've seen that one coming. A quick check in the kitchen—which is a disgusting mess in its own right—tells me the faucet is also nonfunctioning. Great.

The interior hasn't changed much since I lived here. It's smellier, sure, and dirtier. Cigarette butts litter the floor together with old food containers, beer cans, and bottles. My grandfather's shotgun still hangs in the hallway, however, and what used to be my bedroom is oddly unchanged. In fact, it's so pristine it sends a chill down my spine.

My desk, my bed. The posters of old bands I liked and actors I found hot. I left this place when I was eighteen—plenty of time for my mom to get rid of my stuff.

All the more convenient for me. I'm not about to sleep in my mom's bed; that would be weird. Breaking into my old childhood home in the middle of the night is weird enough.

The officer who called didn't mention how long she'd been dead before they found her, but since the house doesn't smell like a corpse, it can't have been long. Are there any traces of her left, or have they already cleaned that shit up? I'll have a look in the morning.

I sit on my bed and stare at a torn, faded poster of Ziggy Stardust on the wall. It's strange; Daniel and I were friends for so many years, yet he never visited my home. I never allowed him to see who I was here. Never allowed him to bear witness to that small and pitiful boy, or hear my mother's screams shaking the walls ... Her tantrums, her torments, her endless slew of boyfriends and tricks ...

What did she think about in her last moments? Did she cry out for the men who kept her company? Did she think of my dead grandpa? Did she think of me?

It would have been a night like this, quiet and listless, when she gave up her final breath, shot full of dope and probably drunk too.

Darkness seeps into my vision, and I cradle my head in my hands. I swore I'd never return to this house if not for three reasons: to shoot my mom, to set fire to the place, and to shoot myself once it's all said and done. One of those options she stole from me, but two still remain.

Before I do anything radical and fucked up like that, though, I need to see Daniel again. He's a bit like Rome, I suppose: all my roads lead back to him. I just hope at least one of those roads has a bridge left unburned.

Chapter 4

DANIEL

THE CLOYING, GREASY SMELL from Sidney's Diner drifts by, mixed with the bitter detergent from the cleaning solution I'm spraying all over the wall.

The irony of removing graffiti that, six years ago, I might have been the culprit of myself never fails to amuse me.

And by "amuse," I mean "depress."

Nathan and I used to have a blast trying out all these different techniques and colors. We rode around like maniacs on our bikes, scouting for potential targets. Interstate tunnels. Bus stops. The back of the school. I always got way too into it, perfecting my art in ridiculous detail, while Nathan smoked a cigarette and tapped his feet, waiting impatiently for me to finish.

All that lies far behind me now. It wouldn't be much fun to do it without him anyway.

Once I've polished the wall the best I can, I take my goggles off and assess my work. Only ghosts of what used to be sprawling graffiti remain. The sun and the elements will take care of the rest.

A car door slams shut behind me. I turn to the parking lot, where a familiar red Ford Mustang catches my eye. The driver emerges from the seat, dressed all in black.

No ... No, no, no. Shit. All weekend, part of me hoped meeting Nathan on the patio was a figment of my drunken mind, but this proves otherwise.

He's here. He's really here.

He saunters toward me in his confident, languid gait, hands in the pockets of his unbuttoned leather jacket. Underneath is a tight, semitransparent shirt. When the sunlight hits right, I spot a glimpse of his nipples beneath the fabric.

Goddamn, he's hot, and he knows it. Fuck him.

No, *don't* fuck him. Kill him. Yeah, that's right. I'd sooner kill him than let him kick me back into the hole I've just managed to crawl out of. I'm supposed to get over him, for fuck's sake. Him being *here* sure puts a wrench in that plan.

"Sexy getup you've got there," he says, nodding at my bright-yellow coveralls.

"Gonna stalk me at work too?"

He tilts his head and gives a lazy smile. "Who said anything about stalking? I'm just exploring the area. Reliving lost memories and all that."

"Don't lie."

"Okay, fine. I was gonna see if the burgers at this place are as greasy as I remember."

"They're worse."

"I'll see about that." He turns and walks toward the entrance of Sidney's.

Wait, he's leaving? And why does that feel so wrong all of a sudden?

"Hey!" I call after him. "If you think you can just show up here and pull the rug out from under me, you're wrong. I have a life here now."

He turns around and crosses his arms. "A life? Now, let's be honest."

"I have friends. *Other* friends."

"Is that right?" He sways on his feet, gravel crunching under the soles of his combat boots. "Well, that's a shame. Since I'm here and all, I thought we could reconnect."

"Reconnect?" I scoff. "And do what exactly? Deal weed and beer to high school kids?" It's hardly the most out-there thing we did together, but it's the first that pops into my mind.

"Nah, man. Nothing like that." He grins, wide and bright. "Unless you're *real* strapped for cash."

I fight to keep in a snort of laughter, and a cough comes out instead. "Well, I'm not. So I don't need you."

"Is that so, Daniel? You don't need me?" Eyebrows raised, he takes a step forward and gives me a slow once-over, gaze sliding up and down my body. "Admit it—you want me. You want me back."

Wait, what does he mean by that? *You want me back* ... Does he mean as a friend, or ...

Before I have time to recoil, he reaches out a hand and squeezes my bicep. "These are new." He proceeds to ruffle my shortly cut hair. "This too."

I push his hand off. "It's been five years. You thought I wouldn't have changed?"

"No." A shadow passes over his face as he adds, "I've changed too."

"And how exactly have you changed?"

In many ways, he seems the same as he's always been. His gaze is just as piercing. His smell is the same, as is his small, straight nose and his delicate, pretty-boy features. How can a person so beautiful be such an asshole? But now that he mentions it, something *is* different. There are dark circles under his eyes I do not recall. His eyes are more guarded, his mouth more downturned. And of course ...

"*Your* hair is different too."

He grins and pushes a hand through his sweeping black curls. "Got sick of the dye jobs. Hey," he adds, jerking his head in the vague direction of my house, "I'm coming over later. That all right?"

My thoughts screech to a halt. "What? No. It's *not* all right."

"Why? You need some excitement in your li—"

"Shut up." Here he goes again, thinking he knows so much about me and my life—what I think, how I feel. I guess some shit never changes. Another piece of the puzzle clicks into place: how fucking annoying he used to be.

"No wonder you're feeling bad, babe, you were pretty drunk last night. Don't worry, I'll get you out of that gloomy mood." His hand reaches out for me again, but I shove it away and grab a fistful of his shirt. Reversing our positions, I slam him into the wall.

"*Don't*. Stay the fuck away from me."

I stand at least four inches taller than his five foot nine, and my bulkier build holds a significant advantage over his small-boned, leanly muscled frame. I could seriously hurt him if I wanted to. Smash his pretty-boy face in until he's not so pretty anymore.

I bet he'd still look pretty with a mouth full of blood though. And I bet he'd probably like it, twisted as he is. One time in senior year, two jocks pressed him up against the school lockers with a knife to his throat. I remember his wicked smile as clear as day, and once I'd ripped the guys away from him, I didn't fail to notice the bulge in his jeans.

"Oh," he says, in a tone that sounds almost bored. "This again?"

"Back off, or you'll regret it. I'm serious."

His eyes flick to my hand, bunched up in his shirt, then to my face, and his expression darkens. "Either way you cut it, Daniel, I'm back, and you're just gonna have to deal with it."

"I don't have to deal with anything. And you need to stay away from me."

"Fine." He pushes my hand off, and I let him, backing away from him as if his skin burned me.

What the hell did I just do? I'm working, for God's sake. I can't go around pushing people up against the wall I just cleaned.

Nathan walks toward Sidney's and sends a glance over his shoulder. "Once you've calmed down, you know where to find me."

I glare after him. So he's here. He's really back.

The boy I waited for. The boy I longed for. The boy I gave up on.

The man I hate.

He dares to come back now, after five years? It's too late, can't he see that? What's broken between us can't be fixed. He's a fucking idiot if he thinks otherwise.

I should kill him. I should choke him out with my bare hands and torch his body until only charred bones remain, and it still wouldn't compare to the pain he's caused me.

He may be coming for my heart, but I'll come for his throat.

Later that day, when I'm home sharing dinner with April and George, I say it. It just slips out of me.

"Nathan is here."

They stop their conversation, and George turns to me. "Come again?"

"Nathan is here. In town."

"Nathan?" George splutters, rice flying over the table. "Nathan Antler? When? Where?"

"He was here last night, at the party."

April frowns. "I don't remember a Nathan."

"He came by today too at work."

"Wait a minute, so you *talked* to him?" George asks. "What did he say?"

April taps her well-manicured nails against the table. "You gotta fill me in, guys. Who's Nathan?"

"He's my ex ... best friend." All of a sudden, this conversation feels like a mistake.

She raises an eyebrow. "Ex-best-friend?"

"We had a falling-out, and he moved out of town."

"Yeah," George says. "And you still haven't told me what all that was about. Dude left town like a hit-and-run." When I don't reply, he holds up a hand. "Fine, fine. But if you want our advice, I'm just saying ..."

I shake my head. "Why he left doesn't matter. What matters is he's back."

"Sure he wasn't more than a friend?" April asks, fluttering her eyelashes at me.

George squirms in the chair, looking deeply uncomfortable, and my silence says it all.

April gasps. "So he was! He's your ... ex?"

"Not ... exactly."

George scowls, as if the memories are just as bitter for him as they are for me. "*You* were head over heels for him though."

"No, I wasn't."

"Oh, please. You lit up like a lighthouse whenever he was around. And whenever he wasn't, like on our family dinners ..."

"... I was bored as all hell. I remember." I roll my eyes, but I'm unable to help the curve of my lips as I recall the way Nathan used to occupy my mind. The uncomplicated, childish fun we had together. The way he used to make me laugh so hard I didn't even have to smoke a bowl to feel high. During those precious years, it was me and him against the rest of the world. Against all those people who didn't understand us. Who didn't love us. Who didn't want us. He slung his arm around my shoulders and said, "Fuck 'em, you're with me now," and everyone and everything else paled in comparison to what we had.

But that was a long time ago now. He might act like things haven't changed between us, but they have. How could they not? He hurt me. He left me. Nothing can erase the last five years, no matter what he says or does.

"More than bored," George says. "You looked as if you wanted to crawl out of your own skin. As if you wanted to leave the shell of you behind, float up into the sky, and go join souls with him instead." He makes a wavy gesture with his hand in the air.

"It's pretty common, you know," April says. "I used to have a crush on my girlfriend in high school."

George gawks at her. "You did?"

"Yeah." She smiles and looks away for a moment, lost in memory. "Anyway, Daniel, what did he say to you?"

"He said he wants to 'reconnect.'" I say the last word with air quotes, mimicking Nathan's casual drawl.

"In that case, what's the issue? If he wants to be your friend again, why not try it? You're both older now. More mature. Maybe he made a mistake when he left. Maybe he regrets it and wants to make it up to you."

"That's ... not what he said," I mutter, recalling our conversation outside Sidney's. The self-confidence in his tone ... So familiar. So infuriating.

Admit it—you want me. You want me back.

Nothing about the mishaps of our past. No remorse for how he broke my heart, abandoned me, and sent me into a depressive spiral I *still* haven't fucking recovered from.

"You weren't there, honey," George tells April. "The issue is he's a raging, narcissistic asshole. Did I tell you he broke my nose?" He points to the bump on his nose bridge.

"Unprovoked?" April asks.

I hide a smile with the back of my hand. "No, it definitely wasn't unprovoked."

"Oh, come on! He was totally off base with that shit."

"He beat you at pool, and you accused him of cheating."

"And you stepped in to defend him as per fucking usual," George says, rolling his eyes.

"And you said something about how he should stop 'trying to corrupt me' and how he 'doesn't own me.'"

"Then he just did it. Bam! Fist to my face. He doesn't look like it, but the guy can pack a punch."

"Well, you kind of had it coming, honey," April says dryly.

"And then he had the gall to finish off with saying, 'Back off, Daniel's mine.' Anyway, that's my point, the guy's a jerk. Remember how you couldn't have girlfriends in high school?"

"That's not true," I say.

"Oh yeah? Are you saying he didn't get all jealous and passive-aggressive? You saying he didn't hate all the chicks you ever tried to date?"

"I'm saying you're exaggerating."

"You have to admit the dude's a red flag."

"I fucking know that, okay?"

"Do you? Then why did you ask for our advice?"

"I didn't, but you're giving it to me anyway."

"Not to mention, he's a criminal, and he made *you* into one." George jabs his fork at me. "A bad seed is what he is."

My mouth tilts in a bitter smile. "You sound like my mom. And Wayne."

"Well, maybe my dad's right about a thing or two. He did arrest him, remember?"

"Yeah. For shoplifting a Milky Way."

"It was more than that."

"I was there, and it wasn't." The memory of my uncle wrestling Nathan to the ground outside the local supermarket might as well be burned onto my retinas, with how easy it comes to me.

The one time Nathan and I were ever caught shoplifting, my uncle happened to stop by on patrol. He ran Nathan down, tackled him to the ground with a knee to the back, and handcuffed him. Nathan's murderous glare and scrubbed-raw cheek still make me see red. Wayne conveniently ignored the fact that *I* had nicked stuff from the store too. But no, of course he couldn't put his nephew under arrest. Nathan Antler, however, the kid from Wayward Road? Yeah, with him, he could be as rough as he liked.

When I came home that day, my father slapped me so hard my face whipped to the side. "Don't think we'll let that awful boy drag you down with him," he said, and grounded me for the rest of the summer.

So I ran.

With a backpack full of clothes and fifty bucks in my pocket, I texted Nathan to meet me at the abandoned mansion on Mumphrey Hill. As soon as he saw me, he tossed his cigarette aside and cupped my face, eyes narrowing on my reddened cheek.

"Who did this to you? Your asshole dad? I'll kill him."

My face burned with guilt as well as the slap. I'd seen Nathan with far worse injuries, and I'd never once offered to kill his mom.

That summer, we looked out for each other when no one else did. When everyone else either beat us or ignored us. George had his jock friends and his girlfriend at the time. I had no one but Nathan, and he was all I needed.

In the daytime, we rode our bikes into the abandoned shell of an empty pool and sprayed the marble walls with graffiti. At night, we huddled up and talked until we fell asleep. We lived on a diet of candy bars and whipped cream straight from the can. Every day was an adventure, and for a golden blip of time, we were inseparable. Estranged from the world, from everything and everyone but ourselves.

"Dad told me he stole a bottle of Scotch," George says.

"Of course he would tell you that."

His shoulders stiffen, and his voice goes dangerously low. "Are you saying my dad's a crooked cop?"

April waves a hand. "Come on, guys, we're getting nowhere. How about this: We all say our opinion on the matter, but ultimately, it's up to Daniel to decide what he wants to do."

I shrug in agreement, and George crosses his arms.

"Fine."

"I say at least hear him out," April suggests. "If he hasn't got anything of value to tell you, at least you won't keep wondering about it."

George shakes his head. "I say no. No way. That guy's a jerk, Daniel. You'll regret getting involved with him again, even if it's just as friends. Just ignore him and let him slink back to whatever dark corners of the world he came from."

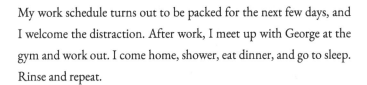

My work schedule turns out to be packed for the next few days, and I welcome the distraction. After work, I meet up with George at the gym and work out. I come home, shower, eat dinner, and go to sleep. Rinse and repeat.

Every day, I expect Nathan to pop my bubble of monotony and follow through on his threat to visit my home. But to my surprise, he never does. I did warn him to stay away, but if my memory serves me right, he won't let that stop him.

With every passing day, my frustration builds. What the hell is he up to? Why doesn't he come seek me out? He sure held no qualms about visiting my house a few days ago. Has he lost interest in me already?

Even though I don't see a single glimpse of him, I can't focus on shit while he's in town. I can't draw; I can't read. All I can do is kill myself at the gym and run until I feel sick, and even that doesn't help for long.

The nights are the worst. When sleep refuses to come, I roll over and flick my light back on, and for the hundredth time, I shift through the photos I got from my mom's house. And I remember my own feelings at the time.

The way my stomach flipped every time he smiled at me. The heat on my cheeks, the uncomfortable, prickly feelings of dread and hope. And I remember how he was utterly oblivious to my messed-up infatuation with him. Or, as I now suspect, he only *acted* oblivious. He fucked other guys with abandon, but he always came back to me. Because we were friends, and he didn't fuck his friends; he fucked mean guys who treated him like garbage.

On more than one occasion, a guy pushed him into the lockers on the way to class, and when I sent Nathan a questioning look, he shrugged and said, "He's just pissed I made him come harder than his boring-ass girlfriend."

George is right; I'm better off without him, and I should ignore him until he inevitably skips town again. Should be easy enough. Given the choice, I'd rather not see him ever again, especially not unprepared.

And yet my mind keeps circling back to our recent meetings, spinning and spinning until I go nearly mad with it.

Admit it—you want me. You want me back.

Fuck him. Fuck his stupid, pretty, smug fucking face.

When I spot his car in the parking lot of Moe's Den—a bar run by the local MC club—I don't know if the feelings that course through me are relief, anger, or a mix of both.

I know exactly what he's doing in there, and I should leave him to it. Let him find another big, mean guy to fuck his screwed-up little brains out.

Ignoring him is what I should do. But before I know it, I'm pushing open the door and stepping inside. At least it's my choice to see him this time—my choice to ambush *him*.

As soon as I enter, dreary neon lighting assaults my eyes, and my nose fills with the pungent smell of old socks, cheap beer, and urine from the restrooms in the back.

I spot him easily by one of the pool tables. He must be the youngest in the crowd by at least a decade. There's the clacking of pool balls as he shoots his shot, and his obscenely tight shirt with frayed edges hikes up as he bends over, exposing a slice of his smooth pale back.

A biker guy with tattoos and sideburns leans a hand on the pool table edge, speaking low into Nathan's ear. He's kind of hot, to be fair—he's got that Wolverine look going on—but he's way too old and rugged-looking.

I walk up to them. "Hey."

Nathan turns around, and immediately I can tell he's not sober in the least. His eyes are drooping, his movements unfocused and unrefined. The shrewd smile he had on when talking to the biker goes stiff when he sees me.

"Hello, Daniel. Didn't pitch you for a Moe's fan."

"I'm not."

He crosses his arms over his chest. "Didn't you tell me to stay away from you?"

"Who's he?" the biker asks.

"You can piss off now," Nathan tells him with a dismissive wave.

The biker snorts and sets up another game of pool.

Nathan reaches for a glass of whiskey by a nearby table and downs it, wiping his mouth with the back of his hand.

"How many drinks have you had?" I ask.

"Dunno. Haven't kept count."

"Did you plan to drive home?"

"Well, I did have *other* plans." He points his thumb in the biker's direction. "But now I guess I have no choice but to drive."

"You won't. I'm taking you home, come on." I jerk my head toward the exit.

For a moment, Nathan just looks at me blankly, suspicion behind the drunken haze of his eyes. Then he sets down the glass. "Lead the way, officer."

We emerge out of the stuffy, sleazy atmosphere of Moe's and into the parking lot. Nathan settles in the passenger seat of my car with his arms crossed, pissed I stole his night with that biker, no doubt. My hands clench around the steering wheel at the thought of what he would've let that man do to him. I shouldn't care, but I guess this is yet another thing to throw on the pile of shit that hasn't changed.

I witnessed it time and time again. Nathan and I would arrive together at parties, but soon enough he'd find some guy to hook up with, and he'd disappear. Thirty minutes later, he'd emerge with ruffled hair, ripped-up clothes, and a satisfied smile on his swollen red lips.

With time, it turned too painful to see him like that. Especially after the unfortunate kiss we shared during that stupid game of spin the bottle.

Senior year of high school, we attended a party at Harper's house. We sat in a circle with maybe ten of our classmates. Among them was my then-girlfriend, Kayla. And so came Nathan's turn to spin that godforsaken bottle, and the mouth of it pointed straight at me.

"Kiss, kiss, kiss!" everyone chanted.

Nathan shuffled over to me, completely unbothered. I, on the other hand, felt like my chest was going to explode.

It's fine, it's fine, it's fine ... It was just a kiss. To refuse would be even more suspect.

He leaned into me, and I closed my eyes. First a simple press of lips, more like a peck than a kiss. Then he grabbed my cheeks and went in again, deeper this time, his hot tongue probing for entry. I parted my lips and let it plunge inside. He tasted like vodka and the sweetness of the pop we'd chased it with.

My vague awareness of the crowd's giggles and cheers drowned in the sultry motion of Nathan's lips against mine—self-assured, indulgent, and with not a small amount of showmanship. Hand on my thigh, he ended up almost in my lap as he kissed me, and kissed me, and kissed me ...

Too late—or too early—he pulled back. With an embarrassed jolt, I realized my crotch pulsed with heat. I recoiled and wiped my mouth with the back of my hand, not quite able to muster up the disgust I knew was expected of me.

Our classmates let out a collective "Ooooh!" while Kayla stared at us with slack-jawed shock.

That kiss changed something between us. Not only between Kayla and me, who were living on borrowed time to begin with, but between me and Nathan. The looks that before had meant nothing were now tension-filled and charged with an energy I couldn't make sense of. Attraction? On my part, maybe. But Nathan, on the other hand, seemed … pissed off.

Our hangouts grew further and further apart. He stopped answering his phone altogether. Stubborn as I was, I stopped contacting him too. Finals were coming up, and I took the chance to catch up on the schoolwork I'd missed, cramming several months' worth into a few weeks.

Next thing I knew, I heard rumors he'd started hanging out at Joshua Tennyson's place. Final term meant graduation was coming up, and I—

"Well?"

Nathan's inquiring voice jars me back to the present. He sways his head toward me, slouching drunkenly in the car seat.

"Are you just gonna sit there, or are we going?"

I shove the key into the ignition, heart pounding and head full of memories I've tried hard to suppress.

Wayward Road is as quiet and eerily dark as I remember, with only a few streetlights illuminating the thick pine-tree forest on either side.

Gravel crunches under the wheels as I pull over. Now that we're here, I should drop Nathan off and be on my way. He's sober enough to walk on his own. But for whatever reason, I fumble with my phone to light our way through the unkept yard.

Knee-high grass brushes my ankles, and the ground underneath is uneven and muddy from the recent rainfall. The house might have been nice and quaint once upon a time, but now it's little more than a run-down shack in the middle of nowhere.

Nathan makes no move to unlock the door, and I turn to him expectantly.

"Well?"

"Don't have a key."

"Then how'd you get in?"

He shoves his hands in his pockets and rounds the side of the house. "It's not exactly Fort Knox."

I scramble to keep up with him and light his way. My flashlight catches a glimmer of broken glass below a naked window.

"Don't tell me that's it."

Before I can stop him, Nathan steps onto an old chopping block and grabs the windowsill.

"Hey!" I reach out for him, but he's already heaving himself up and into the house. Even sober, this is hardly ideal. How hasn't he sliced his hands up already?

"It's fine," he says. "Come on."

Left with no other option, I put my phone in my pocket and take leverage on the chopping block to heave myself into the hallway. Nathan's eyes find me in the dark. He's grinning.

"Home sweet home." He opens his arms out wide in an exaggerated gesture.

I fumble for the light switch, but nothing happens.

"There's no use," he says. "Bills are late."

I raise an eyebrow. "You've been out here all week without electricity?"

"No water either. There's a well further into the woods though."

So he hasn't changed at all, huh? He'd rather live like this than bother doing stuff he finds troublesome or boring. I try the front door, but there's no lock to twist. Strange.

"It's double keyed," he says. "Grandpa liked to keep Mom and me inside, if you know what I mean."

I send him a look, but he just shrugs, as if there's nothing odd about what he said at all. In the kitchen, he flicks his lighter over an array of candles while I lean against the doorway, crossing my arms.

"So where's the key at?"

He sends me a glance. "Cops have it."

"And?"

"I haven't felt like dealing with old Wayne Hastings just yet."

I scoff. "Really? All this just because you don't want to confront my uncle?"

"I guess." He plops into a kitchen chair with his leg up. The chair in question looks like it'll fall to pieces at any moment, the wood dry and splintered.

I open one of the cupboards and find nothing but a wide assortment of liquor bottles, both empty and full. There's a weird, pent-up smell to the place, as if both time and air have stood still.

"So you live here with no light or running water and risk sepsis every time you enter the house. How do you even eat?"

"There were some cans in the cupboards when I got here. I'm almost out though." He folds his knees into his arms, gaze downcast. The arrogant confidence from before is nowhere to be found. Instead, he looks ... pitiful. Younger than his years. Childlike and crestfallen.

"Why don't you get some more?"

He shrugs and gives no reply, but it's not like I don't already know. It's not because he hasn't got any money. Rather, it's the same reason he doesn't pay the utility bills. When we were teens, he'd go days living on nothing but candy bars, cigarettes, and the odd burger here and there. I used to sneak leftover dinner to my room just to get some nutrients into him.

He fishes a pack of cigarettes from his pocket and points to the floor, to a patch of darkened wood. "I think that's the spot. I can almost smell the vomit."

My stomach turns when I realize what he means. "Where is she now?"

"Burned to cinders."

"No funeral?"

He flicks the lighter, cursing when all it gives off is sparks. "Why bother? No one gave a shit about her, except for the truckers who fucked her for cash."

I grimace. "Don't you think that's a little cold, even for you? I mean, I get *why*, but ..."

His eyes narrow. "*Do* you get it though? You didn't live under the same roof as her. You don't know what it was like."

"Yeah, I don't because you never told me." The last bit comes out laced with thorns, bringing up memories I'd rather leave alone.

In this house, Nathan grew up to the beat of a crooked drum, with a mother who despised him and fed him scraps. Beat him, neglected him, and God knows what. He can't be in his right mind to want to live here alone. Not even for one night.

"How long do you plan to stay here, anyway?"

He discards his cigarette and gets up from the chair. "It depends."

"On what?"

"You."

My mouth goes dry. Without thinking, I back up a step. "Meaning what?"

He takes a step closer. "You tell me."

"I thought I told you to stay away."

"Yeah, but then you robbed me of a fuck. You owe me one."

"What the hell is that supposed to mean?"

"Exactly what I said."

"You shut your mouth, or I'll make you shut it."

"Foreplay. I like it." His eyes flick to my lips.

No. Nope. No way. Either he's drunker than I thought, or his self-destructive tendencies have reached a fucking crescendo.

I grip his shirt and push him roughly away from me. "What did I tell you?" My nostrils flare, and I feel like a bull about to charge on a red flag, which is fitting. I ought to rip him apart, slice him with my horns, and stomp him to the ground.

"Fine, fine." He holds his hands up. "You win. But if you don't want to fuck me, why did you bring me here?"

"Because I want you to get the hell out. Leave town and go back to where you came from."

He gives a one-shouldered shrug. "Sure, I would do that, only ... I have this house, you know."

"So what are you going to do with it? Sell it?"

"Guess so."

"No one will give it a second glance in the state it's in. You know that, right?"

"I suppose."

"So you'll fix it up?"

He shrugs again.

"You gonna hire someone or do it yourself?"

"Haven't decided yet."

Someone who doesn't know him might let the subject go and take what he says at face value. But I can see the truth all too clearly; it's etched into the impassive tilt of his brows and the sullen pout of his lips.

With no one to give him a kick in the ass, he won't do shit to fix up the house. Not for weeks. Maybe months. He's going to linger here, smoke weed, lounge around, and do whatever the fuck else, and his presence in town will continue to be a thorn in my side.

Unless I help him.

The key is a no-brainer. If it's truly at the police station like he says, I'll ask George to get it from his father. The window and the run-down condition of the place are further problems, but with any luck, I'll get the place into a sellable state within a few weeks or so. The downside? It'll put me in close proximity to Nathan. But better a few weeks than an uncertain stretch of time in which I can run into him unprepared. At least like this, I'll have some modicum of control. God knows I need it.

"Fine," I say.

"Fine, what?"

"I'll get you the key. And I'll help you sort out the house."

He watches me for a long moment, expression unreadable save for the suspicious crease between his brows. "I don't remember begging for your help, Daniel. Then again ... If it means we'll be spending time together, I suppose I'll take it."

"We won't be fucking, if that's what you think."

"No?" His mouth quirks at the corner. "And why not? You enjoyed yourself last time."

Yeah, right. Last time. We were both too drunk back then, the circumstances all wrong and twisted. And the morning after, when he turned me down without mercy ... *What did you think—that we're some lovey-dovey couple now?*

On the other hand, maybe I *should* fuck him. Hold him down and take him rough and hard like a punishment, a hand over his mouth. Slap his ass, make him cry. *Fuck you for rejecting me and leaving me here. We were supposed to leave together, you arrogant bastard.*

But that would be exactly what he wants. And even though I want to hurt him—even though I want to make him hurt like he hurt me—I refuse to give him what he wants.

I straighten my back, emphasizing our height difference. "Stop that."

"Why?"

"Because I don't want you."

For the first time, he falters, and his forehead creases with confusion. "Yeah, you do."

"I don't. I've already had you, remember? I don't do seconds." The cruel tilt to my voice fills me with both surprise and a strange sense of satisfaction. *How about a spoonful of your own medicine? Doesn't taste so good, does it?*

"Okay, whatever." He pouts, sullen like a child. "We'll do it your way. No sex. Just friends, like we were."

I point a finger at him. "Don't get it twisted. I'm not your friend. I'm not your partner in crime or no-strings fuck buddy. I'm helping you with the house, and then I want you gone. Got it?"

He studies me for a long moment, as if he's trying to work out a loophole in the words I said. "We'll see."

"No, we won't. I'll help you so you can leave again. That's all this is going to be."

He frowns and looks away, and his silence bothers me more than I like to admit.

"Are you really this pissed off just because I won't jump into bed with you?"

"I'm not pissed off. I fucking ... I missed you, okay?"

"What's wrong?" I ask, letting all the bitterness I feel creep into my tone. "Didn't enjoy your five years of freedom?" When he gives no reply, I press on, "Go ahead, tell me. What were you up to, during all this time?"

His eyes grow dark, mouth scowling. He looks like the whole world is bearing down on him.

"Nothing good."

Chapter 5

NATHAN

UNDERSTATEMENT OF THE FUCKING year. My time on the road was an endless highway of disappointments, hungover mornings, and fucked-up encounters with fucked-up men.

I ball my hands into fists by my sides, trying to gather the carelessness I've cloaked myself in for so long. I don't want to tell Daniel what a mess I've made of my life. This thing between us won't work if I let him strip away my defenses like he did when we were kids. I guess I owe him somewhat of an explanation, however, even though it won't be the whole truth.

"It wasn't just about you, you know. Me leaving. It was this place. Shit was fucked up, everything with my mom and that, and I had to get away."

He sends me a skeptical look, as if he knows there's more to it. But he won't get the whole story.

Not now. Not ever.

"Tell me this," he says, "how am I supposed to trust you?"

Trust me? Why does he need to trust me? I trust no one, and I'm doing just fine.

"I don't know. But if you want to be around me, I guess you're gonna have to."

"I don't *have* to do anything. I could just ignore your existence and go about my life."

"Sure. So why don't you?"

He glares at me, the line of his shoulders tight and strained.

I roll my eyes. "God, relax. I'm not gonna jump you if that's what you think."

"Good, 'cause I'll break your neck if you try."

Shit, I believe him. With those arms, I bet he could.

"I told you; I won't do anything."

"Okay," he says with a slow nod. "Now let's talk about tomorrow. Once you've sobered up, you need a way to get your car."

"I'll walk." The road into town is long and boring as hell, and I used to ride my bike, not walk. But it's doable.

"No. I'll come get you after work."

"Oh well, since I don't have a choice and all ..."

He turns toward the window currently serving as my front door. "You don't." Half-crouched, one foot on the windowsill, he adds, "Just tell me one thing."

I feel like I've told him a hundred things already. "Yeah, sure."

"Did you ever think about me, out there, on the road?"

That's what he wants to know? God, where do I even start?

With the grim nights where I'd stare up at the ceiling of yet another shabby motel room, freshly fucked from yet another random hookup, coming down from yet another mediocre high? My mind would drift to my most precious moments then. I'd go back to when things were easier. To when I had Daniel.

I'd remember the most random stuff, like how he gave me piggy-back rides on the way home from parties. Drunkenly swaying this way and that, we'd collapse on the ground, laughing our asses off.

Or how we'd sit on the roof of his parents' house and smoke cigarettes in the middle of the night, conspiring about how we'd get the fuck out of this town, away from all those people who didn't give a crap about us.

Or how once in ninth grade, a group of older kids from my previous school were following us home, calling me gay slurs. I talked back and provoked them, but Daniel ... Shit, I don't even know what happened. Out of nowhere, the kids were all on the ground, coughing and whining. He'd even knocked one of their teeth out. He looked at me with a half-surprised, half-pleased smile on his face, knuckles bloodied and bruised.

Daniel wasn't a fighter, but he fought for me, and when we hugged, he was always so warm. I'd close my eyes and inhale his scent, and for a split second, I'd feel safe. He was the antidote to my fucked-up, anxiety-riddled brain.

Was.

Because I didn't have him any longer. I was a thousand miles away, in an unfamiliar city with an unfamiliar man in my bed, and every time I foolishly let my mind walk those paths, I rolled over, snorted another line of coke, and got the man in question to fuck me again.

You have no idea, Daniel. No fucking idea. But when I try to tell him all this, the words get stuck in my throat. It's no good. He got under my skin in the past, burrowed inside me too deep and too easily. I have to make sure he stays surface-level from now on.

So all I say is, "I came back here, didn't I?"

"You said you came back for the house."

"Well, let's just put it like this: If you weren't here, they would've had to pull me kicking and screaming to come back. But you are. So ... it wasn't as much of a stretch." The truth hangs heavy at the tip of my tongue, but I reel it in. Swallow it back.

His jaw clenches and unclenches, arm muscles bulging with his grip on the windowsill. "I wish you wouldn't have come."

I huff out a breath and shift my feet. That's bullshit. At least, I hope it is.

"You're a shitty liar."

"And you're a good one," he counters.

We glower at each other for a few seconds. It's better this way; if he gives up on trying to understand me, I won't be tempted to tell him anything. Like clockwork, I feel my walls closing back up, the doors to my heart creaking shut like two ancient stone blocks.

I shrug and wave a dismissive hand. "Whatever. Go ahead and leave, then."

"See you tomorrow." A scratch of glass on wood, a flicker of his flashlight, and he's gone.

Curled up on what used to be my bed, in what used to be my bedroom, I toss and turn long into the night. Cold, hard darkness presses in on me, and if I sharpen my senses enough and listen to the memories, I start hearing voices bounce off the walls.

My mom used to lock me in here for all kinds of reasons. For being too loud, for bothering her, or just for being plain "bad."

I pinch my eyes closed. *Come on, come on, fall asleep ...*

The pleasant, heavy-headed buzz from the whiskey is all but gone, and now I'm strung tight like a bowstring, heartbeat gearing up to an uncomfortable rhythm. When I'm like this, there's only one thing that helps, only one way to calm down what's clawing at me like a thousand buzzing gnats eating away at my insides.

Ideally, I need another person to push me to the precipice. It could have been Daniel, but since that option went out the window—literally—I have to make do with myself.

I slide my hand down between my legs and press down on my crotch. I imagine big hands grabbing at me. Holding me down. Choking me. Slapping my face. My cock fills up, and I wrap my hand around it tight as I wet the fingers of my other hand with spit and work one into my dry hole. It hurts at first, but I need the hurt. I need to get hurt so bad that nothing hurts anymore.

I end up on all fours, jerking off with two fingers buried knuckle-deep in my ass, imagining I'm getting fucked from behind. As I get closer to the edge, my fantasies grow wilder and more vivid.

It's Daniel fucking me now. He's pressing me up against a wall, kissing me and fucking me without mercy. He's grabbing onto my hair, forcing my head back until I feel like my neck is gonna snap ...

"You deserve this," he growls into my ear. "No—you deserve way worse than this."

I shudder and groan as the orgasm pulses through my body.

Silence greets me when I'm done. I roll over to my back, panting, and stare at the ceiling with a scowl. I can't believe how unsatisfying it is. Every single time. It's almost too painful: the longing, the sheer emptiness ... I need another body pressed against mine. I need sweat on my skin, spit in my mouth, cum in my throat.

Ever since I was around fifteen, I've had this raw, primal need within me to get fucked within an inch of my life on a regular basis. Beyond alcohol, beyond any drug, that's what I need the most, and if Daniel won't put out, I'm gonna have to find someone else who will.

The setting sun paints the sky a dull, hazy purple. I've spent most of the next day sitting on an old tire in the middle of the messy yard, smoking cigarette after cigarette.

Daniel is late. Believe it or not, between the two of us, I'm the most reliable when it comes to being on time. Daniel's got a shitty grasp on that stuff.

A weird sense of relief hits me when his white Honda Civic finally comes swerving into the makeshift driveway. He emerges from the driver's seat, looking hastily dressed in a flannel shirt and a jean jacket.

"You took your sweet time," I call over to him.

"Yeah, sorry. Had to get this into the trunk." He lifts something huge and bubble-wrapped from the trunk of the car.

A freaking window.

"Oh, come on." Despite myself, I jump off the tire to help him carry it. "You didn't have to do this." All the while, I hide the smile that tugs at the corners of my mouth.

"We had a spare at work. Now let's hope my eyeballing is as good as my boss tells me it is."

We carry the window to my "front door" and lift it against the empty frame.

"Looks about right," he says. "I'll be back with tools after the key's sorted."

"You really don't have to do all this, you know. I was doing fine on my own."

Before I have time to react, he reaches out a hand and cups my jaw. His eyes slide over my face, gaze intense and callused fingers hot on my skin.

"You look exhausted," he says. "And dirty. How do you even take a shower around here?"

When he lets go, my heart is pounding in my chest.

"I don't. I've snuck into the gym in town a couple times."

He rolls his eyes. "Of course you have. You don't think that's more inconvenient than just paying the utility bills?"

I shrug.

He shakes his head with an amused half-smile. "Have you had dinner yet?"

"Finished the last can this morning." The next second, my stomach growls.

"Let's go," he says and cocks his head toward the road. "We'll get you your car and a meal."

"Okay, Dad." We move toward the driveway. I get hold of my cigarette packet and fish out a prerolled joint. After lighting it, I take a drag and hand it to Daniel.

"No, thanks," he says. "I quit."

I turn around and walk backward in front of him, exhaling a cloud of smoke in his face. "You wanna know what I think?"

"Not really."

"I think you've been hanging out far too much with George."

Annoyance flickers across his face. "How so?"

"You're too ..." I wave my hand at him, all of him. "... uptight and serious. I gotta show you how to have fun again."

"Is that so?"

"For sure. You look good though. Real good." I give him a deliberate glance, sliding my gaze up and down his body. He really does look good with a bit more weight on him. The jean jacket he's wearing stretches tight across his shoulders, and he's got a new confidence to his stride. The hair's still throwing me off though. With it cut short like that, he looks more like a jock than the hippie stoner I remember. "But you look far too ... healthy and shit. Gotta hop back on that weed habit, get that jaded look in your eyes again."

"Really?" he says doubtfully. "And you're gonna help me with all this?"

"'Course I will. What are friends for?"

"We're not friends," he says, but the twinkle in those baby-blue eyes can't fool me. He enjoys this. He can barely keep himself from smiling. It won't be long before I have him throwing his head back and punching my shoulder with seized-up laughter. Just wait.

When we arrive in town, I'm hungry enough to eat just about anything. We park outside Albany Steakhouse—the only semblance of fine dining Springvale has to offer.

"You won't get a meal here under twenty bucks," Daniel says.

"No worries, babe. I'll pay."

"This is not a date, you know," he grumbles.

"Didn't say it was. You saying two guys can't go out for dinner together?"

"Let's just go inside."

It's quiet this time of day, frequented only by a couple of stray truckers and a group of younger guys at the bar. Daniel and I settle down at a corner table, and when my order arrives, I wolf it down as if someone's gonna take my plate away. I get mayo all over my fingers and lick them clean one by one with a wet pop. Meal finished, I lean back with a contented sigh and close my eyes.

"What are you all smiley for?" Daniel asks.

"Maybe I'm happy. I'm not hungry anymore. I'm nice and warm." I open my eyes, pinning him with my gaze. "And I have my friend back."

He stabs at his own half-eaten steak. "It's not as easy as that."

"Why not? It's like I've always said—you think too much, Daniel. Stop overcomplicating shit that doesn't have to be so complicated. Sometimes you just gotta go with the flow." I wave my glass of Coke through the air to underline my point.

"I told you, we're not friends."

"See? This proves my point." I fold a leg underneath myself and point at him with my fork. "George *has* been a bad influence on you."

"He'd say the same about you."

"Oh, I know exactly what George would say about all this. Just wait, he's gonna freak out when you tell him."

"He already knows you're back in town."

I wiggle my eyebrows. "But does he know about *us*?"

"There's nothing to tell. I'm just helping you with the house so you can leave." His tone is calm on the surface, but I hear the underlying anger.

I roll my eyes and mash a couple of stray peas into mush on my plate. This new, uptight Daniel is starting to piss me off. I can play the long game, sure, but he's gotta give me something to work with.

Our friendship in the past used to be so easy. We both wanted the same thing: to have fun. We got up to all kinds of crazy shit, and while age has somewhat mellowed *me* out too, I thought … Frankly, I don't know what I thought. All I know is he used to be more focused on having fun and avoiding responsibilities, like me. I guess that's what age does to people: makes them all boring and stable. Smothers the flame in their hearts and hooks them onto the painfully mundane shit that makes me want to choke on a bullet, like kids, a white picket fence, and a stable job. My own flame still burns bright and hot though. For better or for worse.

Where he used to be an open book, this Daniel has his hackles drawn right up to his chin. How do I get him to soften up to me, and dissolve this cloud of anger around us? How do I make him smile at me instead of giving me that distrustful glare?

Maybe some things can't be mended. Maybe I have burned all my bridges after all. Maybe I should leave this place again and go back to where I came from. But that's the thing: I don't have anywhere to return to. For all that I despised it during my childhood, Springvale is my endpoint, my home base. Daniel used to be too. But maybe he's not willing to be that for me anymore.

"Is it just me," he says, "or is that dude looking at us funny?"

I glance at the bar, where one of the younger guys is glaring straight at me. Ball cap, scruffy beard. Is that ...?

My lip twitches. "Fuck. We gotta go."

I slam a couple of bills on the table and grasp Daniel's arm, yanking him up from his seat. We're halfway to the car when a voice calls from behind.

"Hey! Hey, Antler!"

I curse and turn around. Joshua Tennyson staggers toward us. He looks drunk as shit. Great.

"Yeah, what's up?" I ask casually, hands in my pockets.

Five years has done him no good. He was a tweaker at eighteen, but now he looks the part of a full-blown junkie: eyes and cheeks sunken in, jaw covered by patches of scruffy beard.

"You've got a lotta nerve to show your face in town, Antler. What's it you owe me? Four grand, interest excluded?"

"I ain't paying you shit. Come on, Daniel," I say and turn to the car, but he doesn't move.

"Nate, what's going on?"

"Oh?" Joshua barks out a laugh. "He didn't tell you he skipped town with four grand worth of drug money in his trunk? I let you off the hook, Hastings, 'cause this was between me and him. But maybe I should hold you accountable too? You were always his little accomplice bitch."

Daniel stiffens next to me, gravel crunching under his shoes. "We don't want any trouble."

"Yeah well, you've got it already," Joshua says.

I sneer at him. "You weren't this feisty when I was sucking your dick behind the principal's office."

"Fucking faggot," he spits and lunges at me.

Daniel steps ahead, blocking him. "Hey, no need for that. We'll get you the money."

Joshua glares up at him, no doubt sizing up his own scrawny frame to Daniel's bulky six foot three. "I ain't letting you off the hook this easily," he says, nodding to me. "I should teach you a lesson. I know a couple guys who would love to rough you up."

"I told you, there's no need," Daniel says. "We'll get you the money."

"Plus interest."

"Plus interest."

"Fucking hell," I hiss to Daniel. "Not much for negotiating, are you?"

Joshua points a threatening finger at me. "Don't push." He turns around and staggers back into the steakhouse, likely to order another beer.

I push my hands into my pockets and give Daniel a sideways smile. "That went well."

He spins to me, and the glare he pierces me with has me take a step back. "*Went well?* When were you gonna tell me you owed Joshua Tennyson four grand?"

I wave a dismissive hand in the air. "Didn't think he'd still be around, honest! Dude's sketchy as hell. I thought he would've OD'd by now or gotten run over by a truck or something. Anyway, I can handle him."

"Didn't look like it. Tell me what went down between you two."

I purse my lips, shuffling my foot against the pavement. "I was selling off some of his pills and speed right before I left town. Couldn't get a hold of him before I was leaving, so I brought the money with me. No big deal." It isn't exactly a lie, but it's not the whole truth either. Without that money, I would've been hard-pressed to make it my first couple of weeks on the road. "Anyway, that shit's forever ago. Statute of limitations and all that."

Daniel shakes his head, chuckling in disbelief. "I can't fucking believe you. Then again, I don't know what I expected. Do you know what kind of friends Joshua Tennyson has?"

I evade his gaze and mutter, "Those biker dudes."

"Yeah." He sighs, rubbing at his face. Some of the tension bleeds out of him, and he glances at me between two fingers. "I didn't know you sucked him off."

"There are a lot of things you don't know, Daniel." My darkly spoken words land like an anvil between us, splintering the tentative camaraderie I've tried to rebuild.

It's true though. He has no idea what I've been through. And that truth will continue to widen the divide between us until nothing remains but a dark, lonely shore, where I'll watch him sail as far away from me as possible. And I wouldn't blame him.

I clench my fists, cursing my stubbornness and the pain that made me this way.

With a new sort of finality to his tone, Daniel says, "Is this what it's going to be like with you? This ... this drama? This arrogant fucking facade of yours, getting us both into trouble?"

I cut my gaze back up to him, and my tongue twists my words into an arrogant drawl. "Come on, it was kind of fun, though, wasn't it?"

"No, it wasn't."

"But you liked it at least a little bit, didn't you?"

"Here's the thing: We had fun as kids, all right, but before you showed up, I was trying to stay out of that shit. I was trying to get my life together!"

"Well, you're not doing that good of a job," I mutter. Shit, why did I say that? Why can I never keep my mouth shut?

"You know what?" Daniel snaps. "I did what I set out to do today. I got you back to your car. I'm done."

Wait ... *I'm done?* What the hell does he mean by that?

"Okay, but ... We'll see each other later, right?"

He just sends me a tired glance, slides into the seat of his car, and drives away. I look after him as he disappears, wondering why shit always seems to fall apart around me.

If he was serious—if he's really done with me for good—then there's no longer any point to anything.

Chapter 6

DANIEL

THE FINAL PIECE OF the puzzle clicks into place: *This* is what it's like to hang out with Nathan.

His arrogance? His unrivaled knack of pissing me off? That's just the start of it. His magnetism for trouble follows soon after, and while it used to excite me as a teen, it now rubs me the wrong way.

We used to get into these kinds of situations all the time, with varying degrees of danger and lawlessness. It sort of comes with the price of being Nathan's friend, for better or for worse. I've had years now of trying to walk the straight and narrow. Years of trying to make something honest of my life.

And the worst of it? He's right; I *did* like it. It's been a long time since I felt as alive as I did just then.

I clench my hands around the steering wheel and take a sharp turn onto the main road. I see Nathan staring after me in the rearview mirror, and the sight hits me with an odd sense of guilt.

He doesn't deserve my sympathy. There's something dark and twisted in him that he hasn't matured out of. I cannot fucking believe the way he acted. You don't fuck around with tweakers like Joshua; you just don't. He could've had a knife on him, or a gun, and he sure didn't look like he'd hesitate to use it. But of course, Nathan has never cared what danger he puts himself in. Or the danger he puts *me* in.

Why did I take him to dinner to begin with? I shouldn't care if he lives on canned food, cigarettes, and coffee, or if he fucking starves. And I shouldn't care if he has to walk by the side of the road for an hour to get into town.

I shouldn't care about his well-being at all, and he clearly doesn't care about mine.

Right now, all I want is to get home, fall into bed, and forget this day ever happened. Forget how mine and Nathan's lives are now entangled in ways I didn't plan for, and under more dangerous circumstances. I'm an accomplice now, damn it. Joshua knows me. If Nathan leaves town before paying that debt, Joshua will come to me to collect it.

The clock is nearing eleven when I get home. I pass the living room, where George and April are huddled up watching TV.

"Late day at work?" George asks over his shoulder.

"I wasn't at work; I was with Nathan." I'll have to tell them sometime, anyway. Might as well be tonight.

"*With* him?" George stands up, rounds the couch, and leans on the backrest with his arms crossed. "What's that supposed to mean?"

"We had ... dinner." Since I don't want him to completely go off on me, I neglect to mention the skirmish with Joshua. This is going to be bad enough as it is.

George blinks, and his face twists in disbelief and anger. "Excuse me? I thought you were supposed to stay away from that guy!"

"Yeah, but you know how he is. He'll never get his mom's house in order unless he has someone to kick him in the ass."

"So now you're *helping* him? Daniel, what the fuck?"

"I told you. I'm not doing it out of the goodness of my fucking heart, I'm just helping him with the house so he'll get the hell out of here."

"And taking him to dinner!"

I open my mouth to argue, but this day has been too goddamn exhausting already, so instead I say, "Look, I need you to do me a favor."

"Depends. Is it a favor for you or a favor for him?"

"The cops have the key to his house. Could you talk to Wayne and get it for me?"

"Get it for *him*, you mean." George lets out a deep, long-suffering sigh. "Don't you remember how fucking crushed you were last time he got out of dodge?"

"This won't be like last time."

"So you say."

"I want him gone, same as you."

"Is that right? Is that really why you're doing this?"

"Why else would I be doing it?"

George looks at me for a long while, pulls his lips between his teeth, and nods. "Fine. I'll have it done tomorrow."

Thank God. Although I don't share the same aversion to my uncle as Nathan does, I'd rather avoid him if I can help it. "Thanks. You can leave it on the counter; I'll bring it to him."

"Why run around doing his errands? He can come get it himself."

April pipes up from the couch. "He can come to the party on Friday."

"He can come," George says, voice tight, "but not to the party."

"Don't be rude, honey. He's Daniel's friend; of course he can come to the party."

"Really," I say, "it's not needed. And he's not my friend."

"Yeah, honey," George tells April, "you don't know what he's like. You don't want him at our party."

"If Daniel likes him, I'm sure he's not that bad."

"I don't ... *like* him."

George rolls his eyes. "Yeah, you tell yourself that."

When he left town, Nathan abandoned me as well as his phone number. I should've asked him for his new one, but then again, he used to be notorious for never answering texts and calls. And since I've already scoured the web for his social media a hundred times in the past few years and come up empty, my only option is to drive out to his house.

In the car, I think of the way he gazed after me in that parking lot after our dinner. Now that my anger has had a few days to cool off, guilt takes its place. But why should I feel sorry for him? He's made it quite clear that the only thing he wants with me is to fuck me. Those sad puppy eyes were simply a result of him watching his chances for a hookup slip away.

And yet, days later, I cannot stop thinking about him, alone in that house full of ghosts.

For old times' sake, I allow myself to ponder. Is he eating all right? How is he doing—truly? How is he coping with his mother's death? The nature of their relationship aside, her passing has to affect him on some plane.

I park on the patch of grass behind his red-and-black Ford Mustang. He's home, then. Not at Moe's or anywhere else he can go looking for trouble. The thought of him giving himself away to sleazy old men twice his age makes me want to punch something.

I settle for slamming the car door shut and pushing my hands into my pockets as I walk up the overgrown path toward the house. Now that I see it in daylight, the yard is a total dump, littered with a random assortment of furniture, junk, broken glass, and what I suppose is Theresa's run-down wreck of a car. Nathan and I will have to clear it all up before we consider having a realtor over.

The closer I get to the house, the creeping unease from last time closes in as well. I round the corner and climb up to the window. Before I heave myself inside, I call Nathan's name, but he doesn't reply. In fact, the whole house is eerily quiet, with no sign of any living creature.

"Nate?" I look into the two bedrooms—first Nathan's old boy's room to the right, and then into what I assume used to be his mom's bedroom. Opposite the double bed is a huge ancient-looking cabinet. A sliver of sunlight shines in from a dirty window, and dust motes dance in the air.

I turn to the kitchen, and there he is, back turned, cross-legged on the floor with his hands in his lap as if he's meditating. A shiver runs down my spine as I realize where he's sitting.

The darkened patch of wood.

I think that's the spot, he said.

"What are you doing?" My unease grows when he gives no sign of attention. It's like he didn't even hear me.

What's going on with him? Is he angry with me? Is that it? Is this some sort of passive-aggressive way of showing it, similar to that childish mood he used to embody when things weren't going his way? Like when I didn't cancel my plans with George last second just because Nathan came around. Or like when he wanted us to get deeper into the drug trade, and I declined. His familiar pouting would turn to a blank-faced, sullen, deep-seated anger. He never stayed angry with me for long though. All it took was for me to show up with my bike and offer him a cigarette, and we'd be friends again.

I flick the light switch to my right. The lone bulb in the ceiling flickers and comes to life. "Finally bothered to pay the bill, huh?" When he still doesn't reply, I walk over to him and put a hand on his shoulder. "Nathan."

He turns his head. "What do you want?" He looks pale and hollow-eyed, as if he hasn't slept for days, and his voice sounds raspy from disuse.

Don't tell me he's been like this ever since we parted, several days ago? The possibility makes my throat tight.

"George talked to the officers. He got you the key to the house."

"Fine. Give it here."

"I don't have it. You'll get it during the party tomorrow."

"What party?"

"At our house."

"Why would I want to go to a party with George?"

"Because he won't give you the key unless you come. I'll be there too."

"Whatever," he mutters and turns back around.

It feels awkward to stand here in the doorway with him barely paying me any attention. Usually, he gives me *too much* attention.

"We should talk about Joshua too," I say.

"What about him?"

The bored tone of his voice doesn't make me as angry as it should. He obviously doesn't regret putting me in danger. He's still concerned with only himself and his own needs. Always has been, always will be. I wait for the urge to cuss him out, to argue, but for whatever reason, it never comes.

"Do you even *have* four grand?" I ask instead.

"Maybe. But not four grand I want to spend on him."

"If money's an issue for you, then ... I'll take care of it."

"You don't need to pay for anything. I told you; I'll handle it."

I'm not entirely sure what *I'll handle it* means. With Nathan in the picture, nothing is certain except for his unpredictable, chaos-prone nature. That particular piece of the puzzle clicks neatly into place, as do his mannerisms: the way he walks, the way he talks. His sharp wit, his impatience. But there are slight differences too: the circles under his eyes, and the deep, weary darkness that seems to descend over him like a menacing storm.

Again, I can't help but wonder what happened during the years he was on the road. *Nothing good* is what he told me. Finding him like this—sitting on the very spot where his mother died—makes it all the more obvious. I just have to say it.

"I don't think you should be staying here."

"Where else would I go?" His voice is hard, meeting mine with steely deflection.

"How about the motel?"

He scoffs. "That rat trap? I'd rather spend my cash on other shit."

"Like what—booze and whores?"

"Booze, sure, but I haven't ever had to pay anyone to fuck me. It's been the other way around though."

"Is that how you made your money on the road? By selling yourself to dirty old men?"

"Maybe. You want a demonstration?" He gets up from the floor and saunters toward me.

"A demonstration of what?" I'm not stupid; this is yet another of his attempts to get me into bed, and his need to distract himself from whatever's plaguing him.

"I think you know."

"I *think* you should come to the party. And try to behave, all right? George isn't thrilled with you being back in town."

"He's not? I bet he'd be thrilled to return the favor." Nathan grins and grips the bridge of his nose. His smile falls as quickly as it came, and his voice goes low and dark. "You think I don't know what this is?"

"It's nothing but a party. A party where you'll get your key."

His suspicious glare doesn't budge. He's unpredictable when he's in this mood. My best bet is to play it casual and get into the subject of partying, alcohol, and drugs. And sex. Sex always gets his attention.

"It's not all business, you know. Might be fun too."

The reaction is immediate: His impassive mask melts off, and his mouth tilts in a sly, suggestive smirk.

"Oh really? More fun than the time I got spit roasted by two guys in the back of a van?"

This time, I can't help it. My imagination takes off at full throttle, and I picture Nathan sucking cock and getting pounded from behind in some cramped, filthy van. In my mind, he's fully in his element, enjoying it to the max. But something tells me it wasn't as much fun for him as he claimed. I have my fair share of self-destructive tendencies, but Nathan takes the prize by a long shot.

I clear my throat and will the images away. "So you're coming?"

"I guess."

"What about George?"

"As long as he doesn't come between you and me, he's got nothing to fear."

"There's nothing for him to come between. Not anymore." My voice is hard, laced with five years' worth of sorrow and disappointment. "Everything we had, you ruined. You have to understand that."

Nathan blinks, and ... What's that? A crease of his brow, and a flicker of pain he's unable to hide.

"I'm ... I'm sorry, okay?" His dark locks fall into his face as he hangs his head. "I'm sorry, Daniel."

"Are you?" I can't help but bait him a little, but the significance of what he just said isn't lost on me. Nathan doesn't apologize. Not to anyone. Not with words anyway.

"Yes, fuck ... Please believe me."

I've waited five years to hear those words, and yet is it enough? In his absence, the depression that always lurked in the back of my mind surged past the surface. It wasn't entirely his fault, to be fair. He did act like an asshole, but he couldn't have known the effect him leaving would have on me. And it probably wasn't his intention to hurt me that bad.

I can't know for sure though. Goddamn it, why do I keep defending him?

"Just come to the party. And remember to behave, okay?"

His mouth quirks up, and some of his regular old self comes back out to play, eyes glittering under his lashes. "When do I ever not behave?"

Once again, I'm far drunker than I meant to be. When George drinks, he expects everyone else to guzzle as many shots as he does, which is inconvenient tonight, since I planned to keep a sharp mind to handle whatever's about to go down.

I have a hard enough time handling Nathan on his own. Handling him in close proximity to George? A whole other ball game.

Not that I should care if they rile each other up, but I'd rather avoid a fistfight at least. I also have to reassure George that I don't care about Nathan, which to my ire has become harder and harder to prove even to myself.

The street illuminates with a new set of headlights. Finally.

I stumble past the crowd and onto the patio in time to see Nathan sauntering up the yard. He's dressed in a black crop top under a fishnet long sleeve that barely covers his taut pale stomach. As the wind turns, I get a whiff of his scent. He still uses the same perfume as back when he was eighteen, and it's crazy how vividly that smell takes me back and how it never fails to catch me off guard.

His scent melds with the same inexplicable pull that steals the breath from my lungs and renders me unable to look away from him.

It's a compulsion. It's a need—deep and dark and vacant of logic.

It's telling me I want him, that I need him like air.

And I fear it's right.

I hate him, yet I want him so bad I could choke.

"Couldn't wait five seconds to see me?" he drawls as he walks past me up the patio stairs.

My eyes come level with the curve of his ass, perfectly accentuated in his skintight leather pants. He really has a spectacular ass. Round, plump, and with just the right amount of muscle for his otherwise lithe frame, it tapers to narrow hips and a slim waist.

Being annoying is his trademark, but why does he have to be so damn hot too?

I rub a hand over my heated face, ignoring the twitch of my cock in my pants. "Let's just get inside."

As we enter the hallway, April gasps at the sight of us.

"Is this him? My god, he is *gorgeous*!"

Nathan bends over in a bow, real old-timey, with one arm folded at his side and the other grasping April's wrist. "At your service," he says, planting a kiss to the back of her hand.

She giggles. "No wonder Daniel's so hung up on you."

"Don't flatter his ego," George says. "He doesn't need it."

At first, Nathan is blank-faced and quiet, as if he's going to let the comment slide. Then his face twists into an expression I've seen many times before.

"Oh. It's *you*." His tone is bored, but the underline of spiteful rage is impossible to miss.

"Told you this was a bad idea," I hiss into George's ear. "Give me the key, and we'll get out of here."

"We?" George huffs. "Does he need help to unlock his door too?"

"You know what, George?" Nathan points to the bump on his nose bridge. "I think you look better like this. Makes you look a little more world-weary and less like you've got a stick up your ass."

"What did you just say?" George growls, the vein in his temple bulging ominously.

I grab hold of his shoulder and lead him into the living room. "Hey, how about another drink?"

<hr>

"… and after that, it's on to case studies; custody battles, divorce settlements …"

George's words enter one ear and exit the other. All I can think about is how Nathan sits next to me on the couch with his arm slung casually over the backrest. He's barely touching me, yet his skin is like a furnace, sending heat all over my body.

How did I end up cozying up to him on the couch? Fuck it, I'm too drunk to care.

"Property law almost killed me, but this?" George shakes his head.

Nathan grabs a handful of potato chips and stuffs them into his mouth. "Sounds mad boring, bro."

George shoots him a glare. "It's called getting an education, *bro*. Not that you'd know anything about it. What's your GPA again?"

"Not everyone wants to be a good little schoolboy like you."

Oh great, here we go. I take another sip of my beer and try to let their words fly over my head.

"So, Nathan," George says. "How are you financing your lifestyle out there in that hut? If you're staying for a while, are you gonna get a job or something?"

Nathan shrugs. "Don't need to. I've got some savings."

"Of course. 'Cause you wouldn't work a day in your life if you didn't absolutely have to."

"Doesn't that apply to most people?" I can't stop myself from asking.

George turns his glare on me. "I guess you and him are two sides of the same coin."

"What's that's supposed to mean?" Just because George has more ambition than most people doesn't mean I'm without. I've got … plans. Can't really remember which ones at the moment, but that's just because Nathan has his hand on my knee, drawing little circles with his fingertips. Every little touch sends sparks of heat down my spine.

One time at a party like this, Nathan plopped himself into my lap and shotgunned smoke into my mouth. The memory is so intense, and so unbearably sexy, that I have to close my eyes and take a deep, calming breath. My mind might have tried to forget, but my body remembers.

"Yeah, Georgie, what'd you mean by that?" Nathan asks.

George waves a hand. "Just look at the situations you two used to get into."

"What kind of situations?" April asks.

"There's the time he slipped you LSD at a party."

I roll my eyes. "He didn't *slip* me LSD; he offered it to me, and I took it."

"Then there's the time he almost got you shot."

"Oh, please, that was an accident."

Nathan turns to me, eyebrow quirked. "You've really been spilling the beans, Daniel."

"You were gone," I mutter. "I didn't know you'd be coming back. And I ..." *I needed to vent to someone. I needed some way of handling you being gone.*

"Yeah." George slurps up the last of his beer and crushes the can. "I've been there for him. Unlike you."

"Well, you're a shitty replacement," Nathan says.

"What?" George growls.

I groan. "Oh, for fuck's sake."

"You heard me," Nathan says. "You're stressing Daniel out with all your stuck-up bullshit."

"*I'm* stressing him out? He was doing fine before you got here."

"Fine? He was miserable without me."

George shoots up from his seat, and Nathan follows. They glare at each other, fists clenched at their sides. George must be at least four inches taller and forty pounds heavier, yet Nathan meets his furious gaze without fear, a smirk at the corner of his mouth, as if he's just looking for an excuse, as if he *wants* to be hit ...

Nope. Not on my watch.

I push myself between them and get Nathan behind my back.

"Don't," I say, shaking my head at George, who looks like he would have gladly beaten Nathan to hell and back if I hadn't intervened. He scowls at me as if *I'm* the one who insulted him, as if *I'm* the one who goaded him into this.

"You wanted to say something, Georgie?" Nathan pipes up behind my shoulder, voice sugar sweet yet dripping with vitriol.

The other guests have stopped their conversations to stare at us. Even April seems at a loss for words. Not good. I need to put an end to this, but what my drunken mind summons creates a whole different problem.

"Hey, Nate," I say, jerking my head toward the stairs. "You wanna see my room?"

"Thought you'd never ask." With a smug smile sent George's way, Nathan rounds us both and walks upstairs.

Before following him, I give George a half-apologetic shrug. He remains seething where he stands, hands balled into fists.

So much for an uneventful reunion. If this is how Nathan and George act when they're around other people, I dread seeing how they'll act alone.

Nathan closes the door behind us and locks it, then saunters into my room as if he owns the place. I, on the other hand, remain by the door, arms crossed.

"Living in luxury, I see," Nathan says, nodding to my modest furniture that consists of little more than a bed, a desk strewn with sketching supplies, and a messy clothing rack. "This is a far cry from that mansion you grew up in. What would Daddy Dearest say about his son living in squalor?"

Calling my suburban childhood home a mansion is laying it on thick, but I suppose our four bedrooms, two baths, and well-maintained lawn might have seemed mansion-esque to someone like Nathan, who'd have been lucky to get three meals a day and clean clothes on his back as a kid.

"Shut up. It's miles better than *your* crib, anyway."

Nathan snorts. "Anything's better than that place."

"So why do you insist on living there?"

He bites the inside of his cheek and tilts back and forth on his heels as if he's mulling the question over. But then he just shrugs, eliciting a frustrated groan out of me.

I still haven't stopped thinking about him on the kitchen floor. His impassive, broody expression. The darkness that seemed to hover over his very being, pulsing with the faint draws of his breath and the slump of his shoulders.

What's truly happening inside him, he'll never tell. Not to me. Not to anyone. I should forget about it, move it aside for now, and instead bring up the very real, very recent clash with George.

"What did I say the other day?" I ask. "About behaving?"

Nathan pouts. "You say it as if it's my fault."

"You started it. You always start it." Not entirely true, but it's true enough.

"Oh, come on," he says with a smirk. "You love it when we fight over you."

"That's what you think?"

"That's what I *know*."

Fine. Let him live in his delusional little world where I'm still as obsessed with him as I used to be, and where I would walk through fire to keep him safe, even from George.

Those times are long gone. Sooner or later, he needs to learn that.

"You interrupted us, didn't you?" he points out.

Yeah, and why did I do that? Bad habits die hard, I suppose. Nathan inspires a unique blend of violence, fiery attraction, and protectiveness in me, and damn it if that blend doesn't taste good. It's sweet on my tongue but bitter going down my throat, especially now with the buzz of alcohol in my veins.

"At least I didn't break his nose this time, right?" Nathan says with a smirk. "And he didn't break mine, though he sure looked like he wanted to. You wouldn't have let him, though, would you?"

"Don't be so sure."

"I bet you can take him down, easy."

"Well, I do usually win when we're sparring ..." Why did I even tell him that? Fucking tequila.

He gives me a slow once-over. His gaze feels like a tangible thing, licking me from head to toe. "I bet."

"Stop looking at me like that."

"Why? You didn't say anything about flirting. Flirting's harmless."

"Well, it annoys me, so quit it."

"Maybe I want to annoy you."

"Not if you don't want my fist in your face."

"Nah." He smirks, something feral in his gaze. "I'd rather have your fist somewhere else."

I huff out a laugh. "Jesus." I gave him that one too easily.

He turns around, off to find another way to annoy me, no doubt. My suspicion is confirmed when he grabs something at my bedside table and holds it up. "Ooh, what's this?"

Shit. The Polaroids I found at my mom's place. I should've put them away when I had the chance.

"Took a trip down memory lane?" He shows me a photo where we must have been around sixteen. His hair is dyed a gaudy orange, and he's got his arms around me, face screwed up in an exaggerated grimace for the camera.

The next one is of me smoking a blunt, a dazed expression on my face and my long dirty-blond hair strewn across my shoulders. Another is a candid of him in the middle of a party. His face is turned in profile, and he's talking to someone out of frame, eyes lit up with excitement. He's so damn photogenic. Stands out in a crowd. I must have asked him a dozen times to let me draw him, but after several attempts in which he could never sit still, I gave up.

"Jeez, was my acne really that bad?" One by one, he throws the pictures on the floor once he's looked at them. He stops at my drawing of us on the hill overlooking the city. "Mumphrey Hill, huh?" He hums, a smile on his lips.

"Give them here." I grab for him, but he laughs and dodges out of my reach. I get hold of one of his wrists, then the other. We struggle for the upper hand over the photos, and somewhere in the commotion, we lose balance and end up on the bed—me on top, our bodies pressed flush against each other.

I pin his wrists above his head. He stops laughing and looks up at me through his bangs. I start to heave myself off him, but he gives a frustrated whine of *no* and squirms underneath me. Arching his back, he aligns our crotches so I can feel his hard-on through his skintight pants.

That's it. I press him back on the bed, pinning him down with my body.

"You want this so badly? Fine. You're getting it."

I kiss him, hard and ruthlessly on the mouth. He freezes for half a second, then he groans and kisses me back. He ruts against me, narrow hips pushing hard against mine. With one hand, I keep a grip on his wrists as I unbuckle his studded belt with the other. I make quick work of his zipper, spit in my palm, slide it down his taut stomach, and wrap my hand around his cock. It's rock-hard and silky-smooth, leaking precum from the tip.

"I want to touch you," he gasps. "Want to suck you off."

"Too bad."

I'm the one in control. I'll get him off because I want to get him off, not because he's tempted me to.

I pinch the head of his cock, and he gives a muffled groan as I kiss him again. I pump my wrist, only bothering to pull his pants down enough to get his length in my hand. While he's not small, he's smaller than me.

"But ..." He gasps against my mouth, writhing in my grip.

"Hold still."

To my surprise, he stops struggling immediately, and I start jerking him off in earnest. I pump his cock with no particular finesse, only a mechanic quick fix, just to get him off my back and stop him from constantly alluding to sex. I slot my mouth over his and lick into his hot, wet mouth.

He whimpers and sucks on my tongue, cock twitching in my hand. "Daniel, I ..." He licks his lips and swallows against his undoubtedly dry throat.

"You're gonna come? Already?"

"Hngh ... Tighter," he groans.

I'm already squeezing him hard enough to hurt, but I do as he says and tighten my grip—on both his wrists and his cock. I jerk him hard, quick, and demanding. He goes rigid, back arching, and a few seconds later, he shoots his release all over my fingers and his slutty shirt.

"Oh fuck ... oh fuck ..." He races to catch his breath, the whites of his eyes wild and wanting. "Fuck me. Please."

He looks the same as he did at the grad party: hazy, unfocused. He begged me then too. And I did it; I fucked him face-to-face, and when I came, I whispered "I love you" into his mouth.

If I fuck him, I give him a power over me he hasn't deserved.

If I fuck him, I might start to care about him again, like I once did.

And that's dangerous.

"I don't think so," I say, pulling away from him. "We should get back."

"What?" he coughs out. "Come on, Daniel, don't leave me blue-balled here."

I raise an eyebrow at his cum-stained shirt. "Have you looked at yourself?"

"Yeah, but you didn't even fuck me yet."

"I made you come. You should be grateful."

He glares at me. "Grateful?"

"Yes. Isn't this what you wanted?"

"You know this isn't what I wanted!"

"Keep your voice down," I hiss.

"Why, you scared George will hear us?"

"Go wash your shirt."

"Fuck you, Daniel."

"No, thanks. And I won't fuck *you* either."

His jaw drops, and he goes quiet.

I did it. I got the last word. It feels good to win the conversation for once, but not as good as I thought it would.

Nathan gets off the bed and pulls his pants up. Before he leaves, he shoots me a glare so dark and murderous that, if I were anyone else, I'd be worried he really wanted to kill me.

I turn onto my back and slip my fingers into my mouth, groaning at the taste. How can even his cum taste so good? I shove my hand into my pants and grip my neglected cock. I've been rock-hard ever since we landed on the bed, and all it takes is a few pumps. When I come, I think of him as he was just now, helpless and splayed out and panting into my mouth.

Chapter 7

NATHAN

AFTER WIPING MY SHIRT so furiously it almost rips, I exit the bathroom, on the hunt for a drink. Or several drinks. Only, I don't get far before a hand grabs hold of me and George leans into my ear.

"You want what you came here for? Come with me."

He leads me into the bedroom opposite Daniel's. Rummaging around in a drawer, he comes up with a ziplock bag containing the lone key to my house. When I reach out a hand, he returns the key where he found it and steps in front of me, obscuring it from view.

"First, you're going to tell me what you're planning."

"Planning? With what?" I cross my arms, instantly bored. At least boredom is better than the sting of rejection. My jaw clenches when I think of how Daniel pinned me down and jerked me off like it was a damn chore. As a cherry on top, he refused to fuck me too.

At least he kissed me. Damn, he's a good kisser. And his callused hand jerked me so rough and hard, just the way I like it. Maybe it wasn't so bad after all, but it wasn't enough.

"Planning," George says, "with Daniel."

"What? Oh. Well, I was coming back to town. What was I supposed to do?"

He throws his hands up. "You could have—I don't know—left him alone!"

"Where's the fun in that?"

"So that's all this is to you? Some 'fun'?"

"What else would it be?" There's no way I'll reveal to George just how much Daniel means to me. Besides, it's easier to let him think I'm a careless sociopath or whatever. More fun too.

"He just went through a breakup, okay? He's ... sensitive. Fragile."

"What do you mean?"

"Why do you think he couldn't handle college, huh? Four years ago, he could barely get out of bed. He didn't shower, didn't eat. He flunked out of his spring semester. Around the same time, his parents got divorced, so God knows *they* didn't have time for him. I visited him on campus once, and I ... I'd never seen him that way. I worried he'd end up like our uncle Ralph."

"Who?"

"My dad's twin brother. He hung himself in the shower curtain when they were nineteen."

"Oh," I huff. "Maybe that's why old Wayne is such a stuck-up, miserable fucking—"

George's fist hits me square on the jaw. The impact causes my teeth to slice the inside of my cheek, filling my mouth with blood, and the back of my head slams into the door.

The world goes black for a moment. When I come back online, George's fist is clenched in my shirt, and the look in his eyes is one of pure and utter hatred.

"Go on." I show him my bloody teeth in a smile. "Hit me again. I know you wanna beat the shit out of me. What are you waiting for?"

If I can't get fucked tonight, I need to see blood. Somebody else's or my own. The pain of that punch lit up my synapses in much the same way a good fuck would, and now I want more. More pain. More of that sick thrill I get from being at somebody else's mercy.

If George started beating me for real, maybe Daniel would intervene and finally see his cousin for the asshat he is. He'd take me back home and patch me up. Assure me that everything will be all right, like in the good old days.

But when I don't fight back, George seems to lose some of his steam.

"I'm not doing this with you," he says, hand still gripping my shirt. "This is about Daniel. Not you and me."

"Yeah, you tell yourself that."

"Where was I?" he continues, paying me no heed. "Right. Daniel's post-Nathan slump. I thought he was bummed out about his parents' divorce, but all he ever spoke about the year prior was Nathan this, Nathan that. And that's when I understood: It was because of *you*. Whatever went down between you two, you really did a number on him by leaving."

I glare at him glumly, not giving a response. Everything makes a lot more sense now though. Daniel's wariness toward me. His anger. His downright paranoia. I already figured that my leaving didn't delight him, but it was a necessary sacrifice at the time.

"I dragged him out of college," George continues, "and got him a job. During this last year or so, he's been doing well, okay? He's dated other people. He was starting to forget about you and was better off for it. But then you have to barge in here and make every little thing about you and your need to ruin everything in your path."

I run my tongue over my bloody teeth, tasting iron. "You always think I've got some conniving reason for everything I do, that I'm some criminal mastermind or whatever—"

"No, I don't; I think you're a thug."

"—and sorry to shatter your worldview, but that's not the case. I'm here 'cause my mom died, and I gotta take care of her mess of a house. And while I'm here, Daniel and I are just hanging out. Not because I wanna ruin his life or anything. Nothing like that."

"What *do* you want with him, then?"

A smirk spreads across my lips. "Take a guess."

"I knew it," George growls. "So what's your plan? Get him to fuck you a few times just to prove you can, then skip town again?"

"A few times? Way to underestimate me."

He lets out a guttural sound and shoves me harder against the wall. I laugh, holding my hands up in surrender.

"I was kidding, I was kidding. You're so fucking easy," I say with a sigh. I guess he won't let me off the hook unless I let some truth out. "Is it so hard to believe I just want my friend back? Daniel and I had a blast when we were kids."

"And you're gonna try to recreate that now, five years later?"

"Why not?"

"So it doesn't matter to you how it might affect him if he gets hooked on you and then you leave again? 'Cause the world is your playground, is it? Everyone's emotions are yours to toy with?"

I smirk again, but this time, some darkness slips into my tone. "Right."

Fuck you. Fuck you. You're lucky Daniel wouldn't like it if I smashed your teeth in. Otherwise, you wouldn't be smiling right now.

George's grip on me loosens, and his voice goes solemn and quiet. "You knew how he felt about you—no, you know how he *feels* about you—and you like it. You take advantage of it."

"What do you mean?" This time, I'm not faking my confusion. As far as I can tell, Daniel doesn't feel much more for me than annoyance, frustration, and a sprinkle of pity. A part of him might want to fuck me, sure, but that doesn't mean he likes me. Quite the opposite.

"I think you know what I mean," George says. "I know you don't care, but ... it doesn't take much to tip him over the edge. If you think you're just gonna come here and wreak havoc on his life again, you're wrong. I'm onto you."

I smile, savoring the taste of blood on my tongue. "Oh, I'm terrified."

"And don't even get me started on the criminal stuff. He's out of that lifestyle, and the last thing he needs is your bad influence ruining all his progress."

"I'm not into that stuff anymore, I've already told him."

"Yeah, right. My father says a criminal is like a zebra—never changes their stripes."

"Oh, your *father*. Yeah, that's a well of wisdom right there." Fucking Wayne Hastings. Sadistic piece of shit.

George looks as if he'd like nothing more than to hit me again. It won't take much to blow his fuse ... My fingers itch to do it. Bruised ribs and a split lip would numb the bad in me a little. I know that from experience.

But ... Daniel's downstairs, and I told him I would behave. Looks like I'll have to get my rocks off some other way.

"Gonna let me go now?" I ask. "Or are you enjoying yourself a bit too much to stop? Getting you all hot and bothered, is it—pushing me up against the wall like this?"

George surges back with a disgusted scoff. "You're an asshole."

"You and me both, babe. Now gimme my stuff."

He grabs the ziplock bag and shoves it into my hand. "Remember what I said. I'm not done with you."

I blow him a kiss. "Thanks for the key."

I leave the room, mind buzzing with suppressed anger, and worse: the cold clench of anxious energy I haven't yet found an outlet for.

Daniel lounges on the living room couch with a drink in hand, laughing at somebody's joke. Our eyes meet as I bound downstairs. No reaction. He looks at me as if I'm nothing but a vague acquaintance, gaze vacant and dispassionate.

I'm used to guys ignoring me after sex. I'm used to them doing worse things than ignoring me, like calling me a faggot after I've sucked them off. I just didn't expect it from Daniel. But if that's the way he wants to play, then fine.

I head toward the front door with a scowl.

"Hey!" He stumbles off the couch to come meet me. His cheeks are flushed, his movements uncoordinated. "Are you leaving?"

"Yeah," I say, holding up the key. "Got what I came for."

His hand shoots out and grabs hold of my jaw. I try to yank away, but he holds me fast, and his thumb grazes the corner of my lip.

"What happened?"

"What do you think?"

We look at each other for a long moment. I want him to dig his fingernails into my flesh. I want him to yank me closer. I want … I want him to lean in and kiss me again.

My cheeks flush with a jolt of embarrassment. Why would I want that? Kissing is fun, sure, but only if it leads to sex. And it won't, not here. So then why …

"George?" Daniel sends a sharp glare into the living room, where George is reuniting with his friends.

"He doesn't like me very much," I say dryly.

Daniel's thoughtful gaze flicks from my eyes to my lips, and is it really the blood he's looking at now? The grip on my face tightens, the callused edge of his thumb catching on my lower lip ...

He's drunk as hell. Would he even remember it tomorrow if I leaned in and brushed my lips to his? My eyes flutter shut, and I lean unconsciously closer.

The next moment, his hand is gone.

"I'll come over tomorrow," he says. "We'll fix that window."

I lick my lips. "Okay."

"And I'll tell George to chill the fuck out. It's not okay, what he did."

"Whatever." I slip through the door and out into the pitch-black yard.

Maybe me getting punched is the best thing that happened tonight. Now I've got something to hold over Daniel's head where George is concerned. The newfound tightness in my chest when Daniel looks at me or touches me, however? That's the worst.

I slam the driver-side door shut with enough force the sound must carry a mile away. Shit, if this is what happens after he jerks me off, what's going to happen after he fucks me?

When all else fails and frustration takes hold, I need to break stuff.

I gather up every empty beer, vodka, and whiskey bottle I can find. Some are strewn across the yard. Some are in my mother's room, which I never venture into unless I'm desperate.

I throw them all into a cracked washing basin and carry them into the woods behind the house. There's a brick foundation of an old, burned-down cabin here. I used to hide behind it when I was little—huddle into the charred remains, curled up like an animal.

I fling one of the glass bottles into the brick wall. It shatters with this satisfying, ear-splitting sound that makes birds flee from the trees. The act calms me down but only somewhat.

Last night is stuck in my brain, replaying again and again how Daniel pinned me down, kissed me, shoved his hands into my pants, and jerked me off with ruthless efficiency. Even though it didn't happen the way I wanted it to, the more I think about it, the hotter the memory becomes. The thought of his hard-on pressing against my thigh, his viselike grip on my wrists and my cock, gets me all hot and tense. I can't wait until he lets me blow him, or better yet, until he fucks me.

I bet he can take me the way I want. I bet he can pull my hair and slap my ass and feed me his come until I'm dripping in it. I bet he can be ruthless about it.

Men tend to fuck me better if they hate me, as if their anger is some fucking aphrodisiac.

But that's the issue. I want Daniel to like me, and at the same time, there's that sick thrill I get when he flares up at me—when his eyes narrow and his hands ball into fists.

Another issue is my jokes don't seem to work on him anymore. I've been gone for so long I've forgotten how to make him laugh, or maybe he just hates me too much.

I'm tired of thinking of all the ways I can get him to like me again. He can hate me for all I care. It would only be fitting.

After all, I'm used to not giving a flying fuck about the people I have sex with. They're a means to an end—bags of flesh for me to play with and get off on. Sometimes, I even hate them. I hate them for fucking me, for wanting me. I hate them for hurting me, even when I order them to.

I don't hate Daniel. Far from it. He frustrates the hell out of me though.

Another shattered bottle. Another explosion of glass. I lose track of time and space and fail to hear the approaching footsteps before they're too close.

"What the hell are you doing?"

Daniel. Of course. I all but repressed he'd come over today.

Without turning around, I grab another bottle. "Nothing."

"Doesn't look like nothing."

After sending another bottle to its death, I spin around to glare at him. He's wearing his faded jean jacket and brown leather boots. His hair is styled, swept to the side with some kind of wax. He looks good. Too good.

I'm starting to get used to the shorter length of his hair, though I'm not yet sure which I prefer. He looks more proper and boring with his hair short. More like his father and cousin. And uncle. But his dirty-blond hair, baby-blue eyes, and freckles are all different from them. They're not from his asshole father or his bastard cousin. They're all Daniel.

"Did something happen?" he asks.

The question is fair, I suppose. I must look insane with my hand around a bottle and a pile of broken glass around me.

"Like what?" *Like you making me come and then ignoring it ever happened? Like me obsessing over the unbidden fantasy of getting your hands into my hair and your tongue into my mouth?*

I should just be able to let him jerk me off and move on, and not think about kissing him twenty-four fucking seven.

I should drive him away. Piss him off for good. Make him leave me to my devices, to fall apart out here until I go insane.

But I won't.

I want him here. I need him here. And that pisses me off even more.

I hurl another bottle to its death for good measure.

"I brought the tools and stuff," Daniel says. "Are you going to keep breaking bottles, or are we going to get to work?"

I don't give a rat's ass about the house, to be honest. But if this is what it'll take to keep him around, I'm game. Anything that makes him pay attention to me.

I grimace. Jeez, I need to get a hold of myself.

We walk toward the house. Daniel slides his hands into his pockets, glancing my way.

"I brought cleaning supplies too, so now we can really start fixing this place up."

"Fine," I say. "But just … don't look through any of my mom's shit." Hidden among all the dust and junk is stuff I'd rather leave alone. Stuff I don't want Daniel to find out about.

"Why not?"

"You wanna find her old dildos and thongs?"

His nose scrunches up. "I get your point."

We're at work until well into the night. We fix the window. We scrub the bathroom, the kitchen, the hallway. We sweep the floor. We wash and dry the bedsheets.

Come sunset, we go to the patio to take a break. All this work has made us hot and sweaty, and Daniel fans his shirt at his front, shooting me a questioning glance.

"Oh, go ahead," I say with a slow smirk. "Take it off. I don't mind."

He lifts the front of his shirt with both hands, revealing his naked torso glistening with sweat. Without clothes to hide them, his muscles look even more impressive. His wide shoulders, the curves of his bicep ... Not to mention his hands. They're real handyman hands: large, rough, and callused.

He could give me what I want with those hands. He could hurt me, make me feel right.

Heat pools in the pit of my stomach as I imagine it: his hand twisting into my hair, his lips by my cheek, his cock stretching me open ...

I want to taste him all over. Lick his sweat. Feel the spray of his hot cum down my throat. Want him to pound my ass until I see stars and we're both dripping in sweat. We could be perfect together. I could blow his mind if he'd just let me. Why can't he see it?

My fingers itch with the urge to pull him close. To grab him by his meaty shoulders and kiss his stupid, hot-and-cold mouth. To get down on my knees and make him moan.

But instead of doing all that, I push my hand into my pocket and get out a prerolled joint.

"This is her old spot," I say, nodding to the ancient wooden bench we've settled down on. "Theresa. She used to sit here all day long. Chain-smoking, drinking. Going on and on about how I stole her chance at the spotlight." I scoff and flick my lighter. "As if her getting knocked up with me was the only reason she wasn't yet a Hollywood star."

"What do you mean?" Daniel asks.

"You didn't know? Get this: At sixteen, my mom runs away to LA, right? A year later, she shows back up on Daddy's doorstep, eight months pregnant."

"Who was the father?"

"He could be a pimp or a john or some famous actor for all I know. Mom never disclosed that shit to me."

Daniel wipes his face with his shirt. "Is that what you did when you left? Went to LA to find him—your father?"

"Come on, you know me better than that. You think I care about some lowlife who nutted in my mom? He doesn't give a shit about me, and I don't give a shit about him. No."

"Then what?"

"There's not much to tell."

"Tell me anyway."

I send him a glance to make sure there's no ill will in his gaze. Nothing. Only curiosity, and perhaps some concern. I take a drag deep enough for my lungs to burn, keep it inside for a few seconds, and exhale.

Then I tell him.

"I drank, drugged, sucked, and fucked my way through state after state. Whenever my funds ran out, I took on some dead-end job. Slept in my car to save up cash. Once I'd saved up enough, I quit and did it all over again."

My pulse quickens while I wait for his response. I'm sure it's the weed, though that's not all.

It's not like I'm ashamed of what I did during those years. I'm neither ashamed nor proud. It was all just shit I had to do to keep myself from going insane. During the first couple of years, it was like I was possessed by some demon. Egged on by the young, wild rage inside me, and the need to take my mind off all I'd left behind.

The horrors and the good times. Daniel. Always Daniel.

"Do you want to go back out there?" He gestures toward the road.

"Not really," I say, far quicker than I meant to.

"But wouldn't it be better than here?"

"Why? My grandpa's long gone. Now my mom is too. There's nothing bad here left." Except for me, of course.

"Tell me about him. Your grandpa."

"I remember him locking us inside the house a lot. I remember how afraid she was of him." The yard swims before my eyes. The same trees, the same sky—everything's the same as back then. My mouth moves on its own, and words spill out. Words I never meant to say. "She never held me when I was a baby, you know? She hated me from the start."

"I'm sorry," Daniel says.

"Why? You couldn't do anything. No one could."

"That's not true. The authorities—"

"Oh, like Wayne Hastings?" My lips curl into a vicious sneer. "That bastard. He was here, you know? Shoved his dick into my mom like the rest of them. Got her drugs and everything."

"What?" Daniel turns to me. He sounds disturbed. "You never told me about that. Does George know?"

My shoulders shake with laughter. "What do you think?"

"Nathan. I'm serious."

"You don't think *I'm* serious?" I think I smoked too much. The world presses in on me with a greater weight than before, and my heart is jackhammering in my chest. My thoughts flit away when I try to grab onto them. Maybe I shouldn't smoke weed or drink in Daniel's presence. My tongue is slippery enough when I'm sober. And now I can't breathe. I can't ...

Daniel rises from the chair. "Stand up."

"Why?"

"Just do it."

I get to my feet, and he opens his arms and pulls me into a hug.

Surprise hits me first, with a spike of anxiety, followed by a rush of relief. I return the hug, wrapping my arms around his sweaty bulk, feeling his warm muscles against my skin. I close my eyes and fill my lungs with his scent. He's so warm. He smells so good. For the first time since I came back to town—maybe for the first time in years—I feel safe. And I almost say it.

I came back for you. Not for the house. For you.

His palms stroke my back. "Sorry about the sweat."

"It's okay."

It's more than okay. Better. I'm way better now. My heartbeat slows, and my chest doesn't clench quite as tight. I sigh into the embrace as his arms tighten around me. He rests his head on my shoulder and breathes in, sniffing my hair.

I huff out a laugh. "That tickles."

"Sorry."

He backs away. I don't want him to, but we can't stand here hugging forever, I guess. Just then my stomach growls.

"Hungry?" he asks.

"Yeah." The last meal I had was breakfast, consisting of a lonely ham sandwich.

"I'll make us dinner."

I'm about to tell him good luck finding something, but then he shows me a grocery bag. Of course. So he brought me tools, cleaning supplies, *and* food.

He fries up bacon and boils pasta in a creamy sauce. By then, munchies have set in for real, and I moan unabashedly while I scarf down the food.

He watches me with a pleased smile on his face. "Good?"

"So fucking good." I can't remember my last "proper" meal, except for that steak at Albany. For the past week, I've survived on Cup Noodles, lunch meat, instant coffee, and cigarettes.

I wipe creamy sauce off my chin and jerk my head toward the patio. "How did you know that would work?"

"You always used to calm down when I hugged you."

I take another bite, ignoring the flutter in my chest. "I did?"

"Remember when you fell off your bike and scratched your knee up real bad?"

"Yeah. I still have the scar."

"You were shivering like mad and freaking out, and then ..."

"Then you hugged me."

He nods. "And you calmed down. I thought it might work this time too. You need to be touched."

Well, in that he is correct. Our eyes meet, and even though the goal is wide open for a flirt, I can't bring myself to do more than smile at him.

I'm losing it. Off-my-rocker losing it.

"Here." He throws me a lollipop from the grocery bag. "They were on sale."

I unwrap the candy and pop it into my mouth. "What's this? A substitute for your dick?"

He laughs and shakes his head. "You're an idiot."

"Yeah, but I'm hot," I say, words garbled around the sucker.

He raises a brow at me and smiles. It's a fond smile, much like how he used to smile at me a long time ago, and my heart does a weird flip in my chest. I swirl the candy in my mouth, letting the sweet red flavor coat my tongue.

I'm not sure how to say this. I'm not sure *why* I say it, but I do. Must be the weed.

"Hey, so ... George told me about ... About how bad you were doing. A few years back." His shoulders stiffen, and I look down at the table, suddenly finding it hard to meet his eyes. "If I knew you'd go off the rails so badly, I wouldn't have acted the way I did."

"Okay."

"But we were kinda falling off at that point if you remember."

"Yeah," he mutters, "'cause you'd rather hang out with Joshua Tennyson and his idiot drug dealers than me."

A dark, heavy weight descends on my shoulders. "Right ... So, anyway, I didn't know it would mess you up that badly. If I'd known, I wouldn't have—"

"Skipped town without a word?" he asks, spearing me with a glare. "It's not even about what happened at the grad party, you know, at least not for me. We could've kept being friends. But no—you had to turn your back on me and hurt me in the worst way possible and cut me off like you never knew me."

"I'm sorry, okay? I was fucked up, and I freaked out. But you gotta know I cared about you."

"You had a shitty way of showing it."

"Hey, how many times do you need me to say I'm sorry?"

"I don't know. A thousand maybe?"

"Sheesh. Well, we're gonna be here all night, then. You ready?"

He yawns and stretches his arms over his head. "No, I'm too tired for that. Maybe tomorrow."

At least he wants to see me tomorrow. That's something.

"You could sleep here, you know." *Please say yes. Please don't leave me alone out here.*

"I don't know. This place freaks me out enough in the daytime."

"You can have my mom's room. I sleep in the other one anyway."

"You sleep in your old bedroom? That bed's tiny."

"It's not so bad." And I won't set foot in my mom's room if I can help it.

His gaze roams the ceiling and the corners of the walls. "You sure it's not haunted?"

"Don't worry, babe," I say with a smirk. "If it is, I'll protect you."

We brush our teeth and say our good nights. It feels oddly domestic and reminiscent of the many sleepovers in our past.

There's a distinct difference though: Whenever we slept under the same roof back then, it was always in the same bedroom. His bedroom. Sometimes in his bed, if we were exhausted enough. Or he'd sneak into the hallway and fetch a spare mattress from the closet.

One time, I showed up at his window with my face soaked in blood after my blackout-drunk mother threw a bottle at me and nearly took my eye out. Daniel took me in and patched me up with his parents' first aid kit. Afterward, he put me to bed and held me until I fell asleep.

But tonight we're sleeping in separate bedrooms. I hear him tossing and turning on the other side of the wall. Seems like I'm not the only one who can't sleep.

I take a deep breath and get up. My feet pad over the rough wooden floor.

He flinches when he sees me in the doorway, but then he lifts the cover and pats the bed. "Fine. Come here."

I climb in next to him and lie on my side. We stay like that for a while, breathing the same air, feeling the same darkness.

How come tonight feels different from the nights I've spent here alone? How come my throat is all choked up and thick, as if I'm about to start crying?

Daniel brings it out of me. He always has. I don't know if I should resent him for it or accept it as one of the many things he makes me feel.

For once, I'm not even that horny. I don't want sex. I just ... I just want him to hold me. Will he do it on his own? The kind of men with whom I usually share a bed would consider it their God-given right to touch me. But if I have to ask for it, I ... I don't know if I can. I open my mouth, and my voice is hinged on a thin string, beyond my control.

"Daniel," I croak.

"Yeah?" His breath puffs against the back of my neck.

"Could you just ... hold me? I won't try anything. I promise."

As soon as I've said it, my chest feels tight enough to burst. What if he says no? What if he—

There's a grunt. Then he wraps an arm around me and slots his body against mine.

The warmth of him against my back is the best thing I've felt since he pinned me down and kissed me breathless. His hand curls over mine, and his thumb strokes my own. Bit by bit, I relax into the embrace. The knots in my muscles unwind, and some of the cold in me melts away.

I've never really ... felt like this. Certainly not with any of the hookups I met on the road. Whenever *they* wanted to cuddle me after sex, I always felt like a prisoner in their arms. Uncomfortable and clammy. Wrung out like a rag. Impatient. I wanted out and off to the next thing.

But not with Daniel. With him, I want to stay right here. With him, even the horrors of my childhood home can't faze me.

Chapter 8

DANIEL

WHEN I WAKE UP, a warm body is lined up against mine, every inch of skin pressed as close as it can get.

The heat alone is overwhelming. I push the bedcover off our bodies, and with the shift in position, I realize how hard I am. The length of my cock presses against Nathan's ass, and he's ... *moving*. Pushing against me. Slowly wiggling his hips, all indulgent like a cat.

I try to disentangle the arm I've got slung over his torso, but he makes a noise of protest and grabs onto my wrist.

"What did you say last night?" I grunt into his ear.

"Mm?" He's moving, moving, and my cock swells to full hardness. "Don't remember."

I should stop this. I should yank my arm away from him by force and get away from his soft, delicious heat. I should tell him off, for real this time.

"Come on," he gasps. His fingers slide under the hem of my boxers, nails digging into my flesh, keeping me lined up against him. "Please."

"Quit it," I grit out. In one swift motion, I roll us over until he's on his stomach, with me on top of his back. The bed creaks, bouncing with our combined weight.

"Yeah," he groans, voice muffled into the pillow. "Do it." He reaches down, scrambling to pull at his underwear.

I grab his arms and pin them to the bed. "Slow down."

"What is there to be slow about? Fuck me."

I grab a handful of his hair and hiss into his ear, "Are you this shameless about it? This desperate?"

"Yeah," he gasps. "We'll never talk about it again if that's what you want. I'll be just a hole for you. I don't care."

He wants me to treat him like nothing but a hole? Fine. I can do that. Right now, I *want* to do that, and he deserves it. For hurting me. For leaving me. For frustrating me to the ends of the earth.

I push my boxers down and pull out my aching cock, letting the heavy length of it press against the half-exposed mounds of his ass. If I'm going to do this, I won't make it some frantic fuck fest. I'll take my time with him, make him come apart in my arms. Make him cry maybe. He deserves that too.

He gazes at me from the side with half-lidded eyes. His breath comes out in staggered little pants, and with each moment of delay, he grows more and more tense.

"Just use spit."

"We need lube. And a condom." Someone needs to be the responsible one here, and it sure as hell won't be him.

"Fine. My backpack. In my room. Hurry up."

When I return with a bottle of lube and a condom in my hands, Nathan is lying right where I left him but with his boxers fully off, his naked ass on display, and ... damn.

The sun shines in from the window shutters, bathing him in light. The dip of his back, the jut of his shoulder blades, his perfect, smooth ass ... He looks fucking unreal.

He turns his head and looks at me with a quirked brow. "Well?"

I get rid of my boxers and climb back into bed. I straddle his upper thighs, and with a grip on his hair, I twist his head to the side. "You're hot as fuck, you know that?"

He shoots me a blatant, shameless grin. He knows. Of course he knows.

Then I say, "You're beautiful," and his grin falters, replaced by a blush I don't let him hide.

I run my hands down his taut little waist. The head of my cock pokes between his ass cheeks, not quite reaching his hole. I let him feel my hardness as I rock against him, smearing precum on his hot skin.

He shudders and groans. "Daniel, fuck ..."

"Now," I say, pushing his messy, sweaty bangs out of his face. "What do you want me to do with you?"

"I want you to fuck me so hard I forget my own name, that's what."

Yeah, that ass of his is hungry; he's gotten that much across.

He reaches his hands down and parts his cheeks, giving me the most perfect view of his hole. It winks at me, tiny, pink, and inviting.

"Hm." I let my thumb slide over the soft wrinkled tissue, feeling my cock twitch in response to his groan. "You're a bit of a slut, aren't you?"

He glares at me, teeth gritted. "What?"

I uncap the bottle of lube and pour a dollop into the crease of his ass. "You're giving this to me, but you might as well have given it to anyone."

"Shut up," he hisses. "It's yours now."

"You think I'll take care of you?"

"I know you will."

"Oh, but you hurt me. You don't think I'll hurt you too?"

He gives a pitiful whine. "Fuck, I *want* you to hurt me. Want you to wreck my ass. I can take it."

I thread a condom over my cock and coat myself with lube. I can't believe I'm about to do this. Can't believe I'm about to fuck him.

Again.

Don't think about that. This isn't like last time. Not at all. For one, we're both sober.

"Go on," I say, "grab my cock."

He reaches a hand back and wraps his fingers around my length. It twitches in his grip.

"You think you can take it?" I ask.

"Yeah." He arches his plump little ass and guides the head of my cock to slide between his cheeks. "Yeah, fuck … I can take it. Do anything you want."

I envelop his fingers with my hand. "Beg me for it."

"Daniel, fucking hell. Give it to me. Please, I need it, need your cock so bad, I … *Fuuuck*."

I push forward, pressing hard until I breach his tight little hole. His hand falls to the bed and grips the sheets. I stop halfway to allow him a chance to adjust, but he gets up onto his elbows and pushes his hips back, making me slide all the way home.

"Fucking. Finally." He lets out a groan of immense relief, and his expression is one of such utter bliss that it takes my breath away.

"You've waited for this?" I'm panting as I speak, strained with the mind-boggling tightness squeezing my cock. "This is what you wanted?"

"Oh fuck … Yeah, I've waited. Wanted this for so long." He rocks his hips. "Come on. Wanna feel you fuck me open."

I smack his ass cheek. "Stop clenching. Are you trying to make me come already?"

He smirks at me, but it's distracted and fleeting—a far cry from his usual self-assured ways.

I grip his slender hips and dig my thumbs into his flesh. "You're not just a slut, are you? You're a brat too."

"I'll be whatever. As long as you—*oh*—"

I thrust into him hard and deep. His back clings to my sweaty chest as I find us a rhythm, and the sound of our fucking fills the room. Every time I grab onto him just a tiny bit harder, grind into him a little more ruthlessly, he gets louder—all high-pitched moans and sobs, crying out his pleasure.

"Oh god, just like that," he whines as I piston my hips into his trembling body. "Slap me again. Harder."

I strike his ass cheek with a force that reddens the skin. The sound whips through the air, and he moans, burying his face in the pillow.

"Again."

I bring my palm down on him, shuddering with how he clenches around me with every strike, helpless to do anything but keep fucking him, keep hurting him. I planned to take things slow and enjoy this, but Nathan has a way of making it hard to think, especially when I'm buried balls-deep in his tight hole.

"Oh fuck yeah. Wreck my ass. Ruin me."

The next slap, I keep my hand on him and dig my fingers into his hot, quivering flesh. I rake him harshly with my nails, as if I'm trying to leave a mark for all the men who have had him before and the ones who might have him in the future. He should remember this, should remember us ...

"Oh god ... That feels so fucking good, don't stop."

I don't *want* to stop, but the pressure building in my groin will demand release sooner or later. I lift him onto his knees and keep him upright, pounding into him so hard the bed shakes as I rake my nails down his sides. He cries out and goes slack, upper body collapsing onto the bed. I keep pounding into him, mere seconds from bursting.

He gazes back at me. "Pull out and come on my hole."

Holy fuck. I pull out and rip the condom off, and a couple of frantic strokes of my hand later, I'm coming. Pleasure shoots through me, zinging up my spine and pulsing through my balls as I shoot enough for several loads. It goes everywhere, painting Nathan's ass and the small of his back, trickling between his buttocks, and coating his hole like he begged for. I want to smear my cum over his cheeks—want to cover him all over and have him walk around drenched in my scent.

My nostrils flare at the sudden possessive urge I'm not entitled to in the least. He's not mine. Perhaps he'll never be mine.

I rest a hand between his shoulder blades as I catch my breath.

"Did you come?" For some reason, I feel I need to make sure.

He turns around and gives me a slow, salacious grin. "What else could I do when you started ripping into me like the Big Bad Wolf?"

"Sorry about that."

"Don't be. I fucking loved it."

"We should put ointment on it or something."

"Nah. I wanna feel it."

I'll at least clean him up and inspect the damage. Still naked, I hobble into the bathroom and wet a towel with lukewarm water. When I come back, Nathan is on his stomach again. His buttocks are bright red from the spanking and streaked with pink from my nails. Shit, I've even drawn blood. Tiny beads of red trickle from his milky skin.

"Sorry," I mutter again as I swipe the towel over his red, abused ass and between his buttocks. He sighs into the pillow and pushes his ass out to give me easier access.

I'll never get tired of the look of that pretty, hairless hole ... Especially not when it's covered in my cum. I lean forward and kiss one of his ass cheeks, and he makes a surprised, whimpering noise. I wipe off the remnants of my cum and the lube, set the towel aside, and breathe a puff of air over his hole.

"You're this red just from one session, huh?" I inspect it with my thumb, pressing against the soft, hot slickness. "I thought you were used to this."

"You're pretty big, you know. And there wasn't a lot of prep."

"You wouldn't let me prep you, remember? So desperate to get my cock." I can see his balls drawing up as he's no doubt getting hard from my words. I drag my thumb over his hole and cup his supple, shaved balls with the rest of my fingers, rolling them in my hand while he moans.

"Yeah, that feels nice." He turns his head to look at me, intense green eyes half-hidden under his bangs.

Fuck. Why did I wait for so long to do this? I could have fucked his brains out from day one. But if I had, he wouldn't have been as needy. Granted, I shouldn't be doing this in the first place, but this ceasefire between us won't work unless I'm the one in control and he lets me do whatever I wish. He might not deserve for me to give him the time of day, but if I can get us to equal ground by drilling him with my cock, so be it.

Scowling, I flip him over and cover his body with mine, and he parts his thighs to invite me between his legs. I kiss his vicious, slutty mouth, and our lips move in tandem, trying to gain purchase on one another. He grapples at me, parting his legs wider as I growl into his mouth. My cock pressing against his lower stomach feels hard enough to poke a hole in him.

"I wanna suck your dick," he gasps.

"That so?" I kiss along his jaw and down by his pulse point. I want to bite him there, want to mark him all over.

"Climb on top of my chest. Let me show you."

"Show you what?"

He winks. "You'll see."

I do as he says, crawling on top of him until I'm sitting on his chest, my cock level with his chin. He looks so small and vulnerable in this position. Willing. Submissive. The total opposite of his usual smug, arrogant demeanor.

I guide the head of my cock to his lips. He sticks his tongue out to lick at the head and reaches a hand to grip my base.

I slap the hand away. "Nuh-uh. Hands-free. You wanted to show me how good you are, remember?"

He glares at me. "Fine." He hinges his jaw open wide, works me between his lips, and swallows me down with well-practiced efficiency. And just like that, I slide all the way into his throat.

"Christ," I groan. "No gag reflex?"

He pulls back. "Fuck my face. I can take it."

"I bet you can." I rock my hips forward, and he swallows me down as if his throat was made for it. It feels like a dream—that wet slide welcoming me inside, his tongue playing with the crown on the way up. He breathes through his nose as he tongues my shaft. My balls tighten, and I can tell I'll come pretty quickly if he keeps this pace up. I grip a fistful of his hair and tilt his head up as I drive my hips into him. It must be difficult at this angle, but he takes it like a champ, gripping the back of my thighs and pressing me deeper.

"You ready?" I groan. "Gonna come down that throat of yours."

He blinks, which I assume means yes, as he keeps bobbing his head at a steady, tantalizing pace.

I don't miss the smug glint in his eyes before I throw my head back and come, shooting deep into his magnificent throat.

For those precious moments of my orgasm, the world ceases to exist, and when I come back, Nathan has pulled off my cock and has his mouth full of my release. I climb back down his body and kiss him again, and he pushes my cum back into my mouth. We let it swirl back and forth between us for an undefined stretch of time—me playing with his hair and him moaning into my mouth.

It's dirty and obscene and kind of weird, but there's also something deeply cathartic about it. The whole time he's been back has felt like a fever dream—not just our first meeting—and this brings those feelings back tenfold.

I'm rolling around in the sheets with the boy I lost and the man I hate ... Well, at least I'm *supposed* to hate him. Now I can't help but praise him instead.

"You're so fucking good at that."

He grins into the kiss. "Told you."

I spit a mixture of saliva and cum onto my fingers and bring my hand between our bodies. "I want to see you come, okay?"

"Okay." He nods, whining as I swipe my thumb over his slit. "Okay, fuck ..."

I wrap my hand around his shaft and start pumping him with long, slow strokes at first, and then quick and hard, making him arch into my fist. I grab his balls next, pulling and rolling them between my fingers.

"You liked doing that?" I grunt, inches from his mouth as I grip his hair with my free hand and twist his head back. "You liked sucking my cock?"

"Yeah ... yeah, oh fuck ... I loved it. Pull harder."

I do, bunching his hair into my fist and yanking hard. At the same time, I squeeze his cock so tightly I'm surprised he doesn't squeal from pain. Instead, he shudders and moans. His cock jumps in my hand, and unlike last time, I pay rapt attention to the curve of his brows, the pinch of his eyes, and the parting of his mouth as he splatters his torso with his release.

"Oh wow ..." He gulps. "Shit, that was good."

I swipe up his cum and push it into his mouth, and he sucks eagerly on my fingers. He's filthy while he does it—gazing up at me through tearstained eyelashes, velvet tongue licking my fingers, all slow and indulgent.

Once I've fed him everything, I roll to the side, pull the cover over our sweaty bodies, and listen to his slowing breaths as we fall back asleep.

I jerk awake from a phone call.

The sun's still blasting into the room, so we can't have been asleep for long.

I grip my phone and glance blearily at the screen. Shit, it's my mom. What does she want from me now?

"Hi, Mo—"

"Daniel." She sounds all wound up. "I need you to come watch Jessie."

Jessie ... I fold my legs over the edge of the bed, heart pounding. "What's going on?"

"I cut myself in the kitchen. It's-it's deep. I have to go to the hospital."

"Are you okay? Who's driving you?"

"A neighbor, whoever! That's not the problem. Sarah's out of state, and I thought I could care for Jessie myself, but— Damn it!" There's a rustle through the phone. "The kitchen's a mess, and she needs breakfast and her medicine. Just get here, Daniel. Now."

Before I have time to reply, she hangs up.

I look back at Nathan, who's lounging on the bed, leanly muscled body displayed in all its glory. His cock lies soft over his thigh, and he's got a heavy-lidded, dazed look about him, as if he's just smoked a blunt.

"So," he drawls. "What's up with your mom?"

"She needs my help. I have to go."

"Shit. Really?"

I find my shirt on the floor and pull it on. "You could come with me, you know. I could use the help." I regret the words as soon as they leave my mouth.

I know him. If he were bored and restless enough, he *might* accept the invite. But now, when he's gotten what he wants? When he's all satisfied and sleepy? There's no way he'll go through the effort.

He looks at me for a good long while. Any moment now, he'll shrug that one-shouldered shrug of his. His gaze will be full of disregard, annoyed I even asked.

"All right," is what he says. "I'll come with you."

"Really?" My mouth lifts at the corner. "Okay."

During the drive there, I start to regret bringing him along.

In the car, I feel his gaze on me. I feel it when we walk up the driveway to the white one-story house that used to be my home. And I feel it when I knock on the door.

How am I supposed to focus on taking care of my little sister with Nathan in the same room? With his eyes on me, his attention on me, my brain rewinds to when I had him in bed mere hours ago, writhing in pleasure.

When my mother opens the door, she looks as distraught as she sounded on the phone—dirty-blond hair a mess and bloody gauze wrapped around her hand.

"Daniel, thank Go—" She stops herself, catching sight of Nathan. "What is *he* doing here?"

"Don't worry about it," I assure her. "Go to the hospital, we'll figure things out."

"Fine, but don't think we won't talk about this when I get home. I've texted you Jessie's schedule. And oh, there's a load of laundry in the basket."

"We'll handle it," I call after her as she heads to a car down the road.

Jessie awaits us in the hallway. Her jumper is splattered with blood, but aside from that, she looks the same as she always does. She smiles at me with her big, bright eyes.

"Danio!"

I lean down to hug her. Her shoulder blades are sharp, her body thin as a rail, but she's warm, and she's happy, and she's safe.

She gasps as soon as she sees Nathan behind me, and she starts vibrating in her wheelchair with pure giddiness, giggling as if she doesn't quite know what to do with herself.

"Danio, Nathan's here. Nathan's here!"

Nathan swoops down to her eye level and cups her cheeks with both hands. "Yeah, little Jess. I'm here." He smiles a fond smile. "Gee, look at you. You're getting cuter and cuter by the day."

Jessie stretches her arms out and runs her hands through his hair. He lets her do it, not withdrawing even when her fumbling fingers almost poke his eyes out.

Spellbound, I find myself staring at them, and memories flood my brain.

Whenever she found out I had Nathan in my room, my sister would wheel herself in with a Lego set and ask him to play with her. I remember her shy smile when he paid attention to her, played with her, showed her magic tricks, and talked to her as if there was nothing in the world amiss with her. With him, she could feel like a regular girl.

I didn't blame her back then for her infatuation, and I don't blame her now. This side of Nathan—this soft and affectionate selflessness—hits me hard enough to knock the air out of my lungs.

They turn to me with equally sunny smiles, and I clear my throat.

"Breakfast, everyone?"

We set to work. While Nathan helps Jessie find a new jumper, I clean the kitchen and fry the half-abandoned scrambled eggs. With more care and a sharper knife, I even cut up the watermelon that was the culprit of my mother's injury, and we gather at the kitchen table.

Nathan steals little glances at me as we eat. I'm used to the jolt of heady attraction when his gaze meets mine, but this jittery, exhilarated feeling is entirely new. Does he feel it too? Or is he just elated that he finally managed to win me over? That he managed to get me to fuck him?

"'Taying," Jessie mumbles around a mouthful of eggs.

"Yeah, sis?" I ask, wiping her mouth.

"Staying. Is Nathan staying?"

Oh. Staying as in staying in town?

I turn to him, and he leans an elbow on the table and cradles his cheek in one hand. His green eyes twinkle as he chews his last bite of food, but other than that, his expression gives nothing away.

My voice is distant and distracted when I tell my sister, "I don't know."

Until recently, I didn't even entertain the option, and it certainly wasn't something I wanted. I wanted him to leave as soon as possible and save the destruction of my heart and my sanity.

But now I'm not so sure.

He vanished from my life once. Can I dare hope he'll stay for good this time? Do I even *want* him to stay?

After breakfast, I wheel Jessie into the living room and put her favorite nineties sitcom on the TV.

The laundry room is next. Nathan jumps onto the counter beside the washing machine and dangles his legs off the edge like a child.

I load the machine, almost too distracted to remember how to put it on. I feel his heated gaze on me, the magnetic pull of him.

"We done?" he asks, and I figure I've been patient enough.

I shift between his legs and glance down at his mouth. He looks at me hungrily, tongue darting out to wet his lips, hands curling into the back of my shirt. I lean in, and his lips part against mine. Our tongues meet, the kiss growing hot, sultry, and desperate. He wraps his legs around my hips and his arms around my shoulders.

I pull back. "Is this okay?"

"Yeah," he breathes. "Fuck yeah."

As our lips meet again, I can't help but remember the party senior year. How he crawled toward me across our circle of friends. How worried I was to show the others—show *him*—how much I wanted it. How I wanted it so much I feared it.

But there's no performative tilt of his lips as he kisses me now—only his own pure passion. For me. For us. And yet something irks me enough to make me pull away. Our foreheads lean against each other, and I feel his hot breath against mine as he licks his lips.

"Why'd you stop?" he asks.

"What are we doing?"

"I dunno. It feels good though. Keep going."

"I want to. But I want to know ... about what Jessie said ..."

"About staying?" He snorts. "I thought you couldn't wait to be rid of me."

"That was before ... this." I push my hips forward, and I grunt when he grabs my ass, pressing my groin against his in a mimicry of fucking.

"Told you you'd enjoy yourself."

If I could flip him over the counter and take him right here ... But Jessie's in the other room. What if I can't always give him what he wants when he wants it?

The image of the biker leaning into him and whispering in his ear resurfaces in my brain, and I scowl at the thought of him going to someone else when he needs to get off.

"Am I going to find you at Moe's next weekend?"

"Hm?" He kisses my jaw, trails his lips over my neck.

"I don't want you to do this with anyone else."

"As long as you fuck me good, I don't need them."

"All right." I dig my fingers into his thighs, feeling him shudder and gasp. "Then I'll fuck you good."

"You'll do it whenever I want? As often as I want?"

"Yeah. Anytime." I kiss him again, only a peck, but he pulls me in and sucks my tongue into his mouth, deepening the kiss.

When I withdraw, he makes a frustrated mewling sound. I can't decide if it's adorable, hot, or simply comical.

"So does this mean you'll stay?" I ask.

"I already told you I don't want to leave again."

"If you're serious, I still think you should sell the house."

He frowns. "And why would I do that?"

For anyone else, the reason would be obvious. Too many ghosts are haunting that place, and I've had enough proof of its effects on him. Besides, I can't escape the feeling there's something he's not telling me, though I'm not sure I want to find out ... The stuff I already know is horrible enough, and whenever I think about it, the guilt rubs me raw.

I should have done something—anything—to help him back when we were kids. Having him move in with my family wouldn't have worked, but I could have—I don't know—built us a shelter somewhere, just so he could get away from his mother's clutches. But I was just a kid, and I didn't know what to do. Still, I should have done *something*.

Here's my chance to make up for it, right? If only he'll accept my help.

Chapter 9

NATHAN

I was right.

Daniel knows exactly how to fuck me the way I want. He knows how to give me the sick thrill of pain I need to come, knows how to drive his cock into me until I feel like I'll ignite with the sheer intensity of it.

I can't believe my luck. I'm so giddy I don't even care when he blue-balls me in the laundry room by telling me we have to care for Jessie, which I suppose is fair enough.

After dinner, I walk down the corridor to check out his old room. The door creaks in the same way I remember, but other than that, the place is unrecognizable.

The walls are bare, the sketches, posters, and drawings all gone. His furniture is replaced by rehab equipment. Even the smell is all wrong and different. Still, it doesn't take much to remember the countless hours we spent here as kids.

The hot summers we stayed up all night, talking and playing video games. Smoking out the window. Skipping school. Evading his parents' notice.

"Taking a trip down memory lane?"

I turn around. Daniel is leaning against the doorframe, arms crossed, a smile playing on his full lips. Holy shit he's attractive.

"You remember the night I showed up here with my face all screwed up?" I ask.

"I remember," he says quietly.

I don't have to explain how my mom socked me in the head with a broken bottle. I don't have to tell him how she yelled at me to never come back. I don't have to tell him how fast I pedaled my bike while blood stung my eyes, or how relieved I was to see him when he opened the window.

He already knows.

Nothing in my youth was ever easy. Except for Daniel.

My safe zone. My haven. The only port in my crazy storm of a life.

When I look at him now, it all comes rushing back. My throat thickens. My face burns with heat. It's horniness, it has to be, but there's something else there too: a tenderness I ache for but do not deserve.

The people I fuck are not my friends. They're not my safe zones. And that mind-bending dichotomy is exactly what drove me to near madness all those years ago.

At that game of spin the bottle in senior year, I kissed him because I wanted proof he wanted me. But as soon as I got it, well ... It just complicated matters even more. As soon as his eyes turned heated whenever he saw me, my fucked-up brain spewed up feelings of hate in return, and what happened at the grad party made it even more obvious.

The people I fuck and the people I like can't be one and the same. The people I fuck are usually nameless, dumb assholes I don't give a fuck about beyond what pleasure and pain they can bring me for the night. Now Daniel wants me to lay off the anonymous fucks and have sex with only him? A week ago, I'd call bullshit if you told me I'd ever agree to something like that, but with a tongue in my mouth and a crotch pressed against mine, I'll agree to just about anything. Stupid.

Gillian Hasting's shrill voice cuts into my thoughts.

"Jessie! Where are you, darling?"

Daniel sends me an urgent look of *don't fuck this up* before he hurries down the corridor. I follow him, hands in my pockets.

"Did you leave her unattended?" Gillian kneels in front of her daughter, sending Daniel an accusatory glare.

"She's just watching TV, Mom."

Her gaze cuts up to me, her blue eyes so cold they send a chill down my spine. "Daniel," she says, voice stern. "That boy is not welcome here."

That boy. She says it the same way George says my name: as if it's poison they're spitting from their tongues.

Daniel motions to Jessie. "He's good with her. You should've seen how she lit up when she saw him."

"I don't care," Gillian snaps. "Jessie deserves better than to spend even a *second* with a criminal under her roof. If I find anything missing or broken, I'll know who to blame."

"Oh, come on!" His voice grows louder, more high-pitched, a childish tone peeking through. "Mom, don't be like this."

"It's cool," I say. "I'll leave."

"I'm driving you," says Daniel.

Jessie stretches her arms out to me. "No! Nathan, stay."

Under Gillian's watchful, icy blue gaze, I walk up to Jessie and ruffle her hair. "It's okay, little Jess. I'll catch up with you later."

Once we've packed ourselves into his car, Daniel clenches his hands around the steering wheel. "Sorry about that."

I shrug. "Whatever."

"No, it's not whatever. She shouldn't treat you like that."

"I'm used to it." I send him a tired smile. "You're the only one who can stand me."

"That's ... not true."

"I sure don't know of anyone else who can." My tone is light, but something burns at the back of my throat as I say it.

"Jessie likes you."

"Jessie likes everyone."

"Not everyone."

I don't have to ask; he'll spill it anyway if I'm quiet for long enough.

"My uncle," he mutters. "She doesn't like my uncle."

I grin and cross my arms, leaning back in the seat. "Who does?"

We spend the rest of the ride in silence. Dark patches of trees and a dreary, cloud-covered sky greet us at Wayward Road, and as the car rolls to a stop, Daniel turns to me.

"I have work in the morning. I'll see you tomorrow, okay? Try to stay out of trouble until then."

A sick, nervous feeling surges up in my chest. Part of me wants to kiss him. Part of me doesn't want him to leave at all. But when I glance over, his gaze is too guarded, his mouth a tense line.

I get out and watch him drive away. My hands clench in my pockets, and as the nervousness recedes, a great emptiness replaces it.

Why? I've got everything all sorted out. Daniel promised he'll come here and rail the shit out of me at my convenience. Only ... I don't think that's all he wants.

He wants what lonely people trap themselves into so they can get a consistent fuck.

He wants a relationship.

A boyfriend.

Love.

Pleasure is easy to understand and easy to forget about. I know how to take a man to heaven in three minutes flat. But this? I haven't got a clue.

I'm fucked. Completely and utterly fucked, in all the wrong ways.

The sky reaches above me, black and moonless. Smoke and pollution from the nearby factories drift over these lands. Perhaps that's what poisons the minds of the people out here. Perhaps that's why my mother was such a crazy bitch. Perhaps that's why I am the way I am.

I exhale a cloud of smoke and lean back on the patio bench. The effects of the weed tingle into my fingertips and make me feel light and heavy at the same time. Dizzy. Weightless.

It's eight in the evening the next day. Daniel told me he'd come after work, but he's nowhere to be seen. Maybe George has finally convinced him of what a bad seed I am.

Ennis's dog barks in the distance. The sound echoes in my ears and seems to go on forever. I lean back and let it take over my mind for a while, annoying as it is. It's better than what's moving in there on its own.

Sometime later, Jagger barks again, closer than before. Back when my mom was around and that dog came within ten yards of our house, she used to yell and wave her off. Once, she'd riled the dog up so bad Ennis had to come hobbling to calm both of them down.

Theresa tended to make even the kindest, most docile creatures lose their minds. And I'm not kind; I'm rotten, so the effect she had on me is no surprise.

She gave me life, but she damn near killed me.

"Jagger! Come here, girl!" Ennis yells in the distance.

I stand from the chair, flick the joint to the floor, and snuff it out with my boot. Jagger emerges from the darkness and runs up to me, tail wagging.

I kneel to run my hands over her coarse fur. She smells the way wet, unwashed dogs tend to smell, but I don't mind. She licks my hand, my fingers, and my face when she can reach it.

Ennis hobbles over the yard with his walking stick. His cloudy gray eyes peer at me from the darkness. "You still here, boy?"

"Guess so."

"Jagger doesn't like you being here."

"She seems to like me just fine."

"I don't mean she doesn't *like* you. She doesn't like you being *here* is all. And I don't either."

"Well, where else would I be?" I mutter, taking refuge in Jagger's warm, soft fur and encouraging whines. She sits on the porch while I ruffle her sides with both hands.

"Young boy like you, surely you've got places to go and people who care about you. You don't want to become like me, an old man who no one gives the time of day."

I roll my eyes. Will this geezer give me the same tired old spiel as Daniel?

"It's not good for you to stay here, kid."

There it is.

"I know." The words settle like a heavy weight in my gut. "I know it's not."

"So why're you still here?"

"Didn't you say you don't stick your nose into other people's business?"

Ennis smiles with a broken mouth—half his teeth missing and the rest crooked stumps. "I'm just trying to look out for you, boy. I didn't do it before. But your mama's dead now, and this place is of no use to you." He looks above me, gaze roaming over the house, and a frown creases his wrinkled forehead.

For a moment, his eyes widen, and his face twists into an expression of horror. I look to where he's looking, but there's nothing there. Nothing but an old house with old, dark memories.

He clacks his walking stick into the mud and shudders. "What went on out here was the devil's work."

A cold feeling settles in my gut, and images threaten to flood my brain. I clench my teeth, refusing to let them come.

Damn this old man. I need Daniel. Where the fuck is he?

"If it was so bad and all," I say, "why didn't you do anything?"

"Like I said, I don't stick my nose into other people's business." Ennis points with his stick at the dog. "Now, Jagger here is a good girl. She's mellow as an old horse. But as soon as we get within a hundred yards of this place, she always goes mad, whining and barking her head off."

I rub Jagger under the ears and stroke her silky-smooth forehead. She looks up at me, and those large brown eyes feel like they're staring into my soul. She starts whining again, as if she doesn't like what she's seeing.

"Listen to me, boy," Ennis grumbles. "There's no use dwelling in what's dark and what's evil. What's done has been done. All you can do is move on and seek greener pastures."

I shake my head. "There are no greener pastures, old man."

I've tried to find them. I've tried everything in my power to feel better, to be better. But still, there is that darkness. Still, there is that fear. From what haunts me there is no escape, and what's twisted in me cannot be unraveled.

I might as well deteriorate out here, in the place that made me this way. If it gets too much, I can always take my grandpa's sawed-off shotgun and put an end to it. If everything goes to shit—like things tend to where I'm involved—I have my way out. My exit plan.

Further down the yard, a car enters the driveway, and my chest deflates with a tingling rush of relief. *Finally.*

Daniel walks toward us. Ennis greets him with a nod and gestures in my direction.

"You keep an eye on this one, boy. And you," he says, addressing me again. "Remember what I told you." At that, he purses his lips and gives a sharp, shrill whistle. Jagger bolts to his side, and they both disappear into a dark swatch of trees.

"What was that about?" Daniel asks.

I grip his hand and start pulling him toward the house. "What took you so long?"

"Sorry, work needed me on overtime. I texted you, but I guess you didn't check."

"Phone's inside," I say, distracted by the pulsing beat of my own heart. "Come on." As we step up the porch, the door seems to tilt in front of my eyes, and a wave of anxious energy surges through me.

"Here." Daniel hands me something wrapped in wax paper. "From Sidney's."

"Right," I say without making a move to take it. There's a more pressing issue at hand: a dark and vicious thing, bubbling up from places better left alone. It tightens my throat, blurs my vision, and sends images flashing through my mind.

I don't think about that stuff. The old shit. From before. My mother, my childhood. Nothing more than surface-level anyway—memories that don't sting as sharp or as vivid. But Ennis knocked on the firmly shut door within me, and now clawing fingers are trying to pry it open. I need something to shut it again. I need to narrow my reality down to one pinpoint-sharp focus.

As soon as we're both inside, I pounce, slam Daniel into the door and kiss him hard and full on the mouth. Clutching his shoulders, I press our bodies close and lick along his lower lip, tasting the salt and grease from Sidney's fries.

"What about the burger?" he asks, voice muffled between our lips.

"You can feed me later."

I want him. I want him now. Darkness presses in on me, but I know just the thing to repel it. It always works, never fails to give me what I need.

Daniel gets his hands on my shoulders, pushing me gently back. "What's wrong?"

"What do you think?" I kiss him again and press my palm to his crotch. "I've wanted this all day. You took forever. Come on." I take his hand again and lead him toward my mother's bedroom, but at the last second, I change my mind and steer us into my old boy's room instead.

"Here? But—"

"Shut up."

I push him onto the narrow twin bed and unzip his pants. When I get his cock into my mouth, his hesitation dissolves, and before long, I have him groaning and grabbing at my hair.

I tear my shirt off. He gets rid of his own clothes, and soon enough we're naked, with him crowding me up on the bed, kissing me.

"Turn around," he says, voice husky with arousal.

I roll onto my stomach. *Yeah, go ahead. Fuck me the way you did before ... Use me as your hole, rip me apart, wreck me. Cover me in cum and spit in my face. Hurt me, hurt me ...*

But what I feel instead is his kisses on my neck. Slow and unhurried, he makes his way down my spine, and I shudder with the pleasure-pain of him kneading the sore skin of my ass. He parts my cheeks, opening a path for his tongue to slide over my hole.

I can't help but squirm. People rarely do this to me, and for some reason, I have a hard time relaxing when they do. I twist my neck up, and my eyes fixate on a scratch on the windowsill. A memory resurfaces—voices this time. Voices, and loud music. The crack of a beer can. Laughter. A breath hissing by my ear ...

"Relax," Daniel says, bringing me back to the present. "I want to open you up."

I bury my face into the pillow, shut my eyes, and give a muffled, "Okay."

He grabs onto my hips and tilts my ass into the air until I'm halfway on my knees. He groans as he buries his face between my cheeks, licking into me. Bit by bit, he coaxes me open. His thumbs pry my cheeks apart as he pushes the tip of his tongue past my tight rim.

"Wow," I gasp, "that feels ... so fucking good." I rock my hips and try to lose myself in the warm, wet swirl of his tongue. Something blunt presses into me—his finger, thrusting in and out while his tongue moves alongside it, maddeningly slow. I whine and rock my hips back and forth, trying to get more friction, more pleasure, more pain, more, more, more.

He pulls back and snaps open a bottle of lube. The cold drizzle into my crack makes me shiver with anticipation, and with a deep, dark hunger I can't make sense of.

"Do it," I grit out, pushing my ass into the air, baring myself to him. "Daniel, please."

"Turn around."

I turn around and reach for him. "Do it." My brain runs in two lanes, split apart by conflicting chants: *fuck me, fuck me, fuck me,* and *hurt me, hurt me, hurt me.* Just when it's getting too intense to bear, Daniel sheathes his cock with a condom, hikes my knees over his shoulders, and presses inside.

"Oh *fuck*—" I choke on my next breath, and it turns into a sob.

"Feels good?"

"Yeah. More."

He bends over, bracing his hands on either side of me. His face is tight with concentration, as if he's not doing this for his own pleasure as much as he does it for mine.

The thought makes me frown, but the next thrust wipes away my annoyance. Never mind. I don't care. I rock my hips, desperate to impale myself on his thick perfect cock.

Yes. This is what I need, this is what I need ...

But it's not enough. I need more.

I grasp his wrist and press his hand to my throat. He keeps it there without increasing the pressure.

"Hold me." It comes out more of a plea than an order.

Daniel tightens his hand, fingers closing around the tendons of my throat.

I grab his arm by the elbow. "Do it really fucking hard. And don't stop."

He frowns. "You want me to hurt you?"

"Yeah." Pathetic tears well up in my eyes from how worried he sounds. How disturbed he sounds. "Please."

He withdraws the hand. Panicked, I grab his forearm, trying to put it back.

"Why?" His eyes are narrow and questioning as they flit from my face to my throat.

"Don't you want to put me in my place? Punish me? You hate me, right?" It takes all I have in me to keep my voice steady and emotionless. "You hate me for leaving. You told me so."

He stops moving entirely, and his hand goes soft and slack. "What's going on? What happened outside, with that man?"

"Daniel, please." I squeeze my hand around his arm. "It's the only thing that makes me feel right."

"You feel right when you're hurting?"

"Maybe. You think it's too fucked up?" My mouth twists, and something like real fear slips through the cracks of my voice. "I'm too damaged for you? Not hot anymore?"

He shakes his head. "No, that's not it. I'm just trying to understand you."

The warm reassurance in his voice frustrates me to no end. I don't usually have to convince guys to hurt me. If they don't do it of their own volition, they're quick and eager to obey. No one has ever refused.

Except for Daniel. Fuck! Why does it always have to be him?

"Well, I don't know what to say," I mutter. "You're gonna have to fuck this out of me, I guess." But the dust has settled, and in its wake we're both soft.

Daniel gazes into my eyes with intent, as if he's trying to decipher some kind of code, but it's a code that can't be solved; I don't understand it myself.

"If you're not gonna fuck me, get off me, then." Because if he won't let me escape, what good is he to me?

I hurl myself upward, but Daniel grabs my wrists and pins them to the bed.

"I told you to relax. I want to make this good for you."

"You already know what would make it good for me." Scowling, I buck my hips in another half-hearted attempt to get him off me.

Sweaty strands of hair dance around his face as he shakes his head. "I won't be like *them*. The other men you've slept with."

"Why?" My mouth twists into a dirty smile. "They give me what I want, and I don't even have to ask."

"This is not what you want."

As if he knows anything about it. Fuck! My eyes are burning again.

"You're right; I *don't* want this. Now get the fuck off me." I buck again, but Daniel holds me down, his weight pinning me in place. It's not aggressive; it's more like he's trying to relax the anxious beat of my heart by molding his body against mine like a weighted blanket.

But nothing can relax me. Nothing can get this awful feeling out of my chest, except the one thing Daniel refuses to give me.

He runs his hands along my sides, slow and soothing. I let out a sigh and tilt my head back.

The moon shines in from the window, painting Daniel's strong jaw and broad shoulders in soft blue light. Those biceps of his, those hands that could bring me so much pleasure if he'd only give it to me ...

Time slips away. The pressure of his body weighs me down, deep into the mattress, and my tight muscles unwind, leaving me utterly exhausted. But it's a good kind of exhaustion, like the feeling when you're so insanely baked you can't tell one thought from the next. I feel floaty and strange as I buck my hips upward with a whine.

"That's better," Daniel whispers.

He eases up on me, and I stay put as he makes his way down. His mouth closes around my left nipple, worrying the nub with his tongue. He licks my stomach, the trail of hair by my belly button. He kisses the insides of my thighs, runs his hand up my leg. Presses his lips to the arch of my foot.

It's too tender, too ... loving. Worlds apart from my one-night stands with men who'd hold me down and plow my ass until I screamed.

One sadistic, unhinged fucker handcuffed me to his bed out of nowhere midfuck. There I was, chained to a stranger's bed in an unfamiliar city in the middle of the night. He fed me poppers, rubbed coke into my gums, and proceeded to press all sorts of toys inside me until I felt stretched and sore and gaping.

The flogging came next. My muffled screams only egged him on further. Then, interchanged with lines of coke, he fucked me for what felt like hours.

Through it all, I didn't feel a lick of fear.

I'm scared now though. This is a whole other type of danger—one I'm not equipped to handle or understand. One that threatens to blow open my carefully barricaded doors, beyond which there is nothing but terror.

Daniel runs his tongue up the length of my cock, flattening it against my stomach carefully and slowly. When I start squirming, he holds my hips down, keeping me in place.

Through it all, my eyes are burning. I hide my face in my arm and blink, trying desperately not to let the tears spill, but they do. Oh god, they do. My chest clenches and tightens. My voice breaks on a moan.

This ... this is not what I want ... This leaves me feeling raw and vulnerable. Awkward and unsure.

When Daniel finally takes me into his mouth, I gasp in surprise. My cock throbs. I'm so hard I ache. Again and again, I moan as he sucks me, kisses the tip of my cock, and slides back down to the hilt. A finger nudges my wet, stretched hole and pushes inside. The combined pleasures send me tumbling over the edge, far sooner than I expected, and my cock twitches as I spill into his hot mouth. I buck my hips, I gasp, I shake. A gaping chasm opens within me and leaves me a boneless, tingling mess, and the memories recede to the back of my head.

Finally.

Alongside the relief, a great well of emotions descends over me, and I can no longer hold the tears back. I hide my face in Daniel's neck, and he holds me as my body quakes with sobs.

It's horrible. It's wonderful.

We stay entangled for a long time, until I've soaked his skin with tears and my throat is raw and aching.

He nudges his face into my neck. "Better now?"

I manage a whimpered, "Yeah."

In some ways, I *do* feel better. In others, I feel worse than I ever have.

Chapter 10

DANIEL

I AWAKE WITH THE memory of Nathan nuzzling into my shoulder and pressing a kiss to my neck in the night. His face is half-obscured now, with part of it covered by his messy black hair and the rest smushed into the pillow.

In sleep, his face looks soft and unguarded—jaw slack and eyebrows softly tilted. In sleep, he can't use his body or his words to throw me off. He can't spin me sweet lies or deflect my questions with sarcastic remarks.

He yawns big and wide, his eyelids flicker open, and our eyes meet.

There's a tense moment as I await his reaction. You never know with Nathan. He might be embarrassed about last night—though he has no reason to be—and he might attempt to hide his embarrassment with sharp glares and sharper words.

But there's nothing like that. His face lingers in the peacefulness of sleep, and the corner of his mouth quirks upward in a soft smile.

I slide my fingers through his hair, and our lips graze now and again in the lazy type of morning kisses I've shared with former girlfriends. Never did it cross my mind I'd experience this with Nathan one day. The thought has me pulling back from his embrace, because this newfound thing between us feels too fragile to even think about, let alone speak of.

"So," he drawls. "Now that I'm not crying anymore, are you gonna fuck me the way I want?"

"Are you going to tell me what yesterday was about?"

He sighs and rubs his forehead into the pillow. "There's nothing to tell." I send him a look, and he rolls onto his back, frowning. "Fine. That old man with the dog ... He's an old neighbor, all right? Seeing him, talking to him ... It just reminded me of what it used to be like out here. Back when I was a kid."

"If you don't like to be reminded of it, why stay here?"

He lifts his shoulders in a strained shrug. "Dunno. I like suffering, I suppose."

My jaw clenches at the casual truth in those words. He likes suffering, all right. It's a bad type of suffering—not the one when I have him writhing and begging in bed. Not like last night. He opened up to me so sweetly then, and he even cried, like he used to on a few rare occasions when we were kids, like the time he came to me with fresh blood on his face.

No matter what has transpired between us, no matter the broken promises and broken hearts, when he calls out for me, I can't help but answer.

I need to do something. I need to get him out of here.

He doesn't want to rent an apartment, but perhaps he could move in with me, April, and George. Yeah, that could work. We've been looking for a roommate anyway. But I have to be careful about it—he'll pull his defenses up high if he sniffs out the barest hint of pity.

"You could move in with us, you know," I say slowly. "We've got a spare room."

He snorts. "With you and George?"

Right. Bad idea. The chances of George allowing him to move in are as slim as the chances of them getting along, but it's worth a try.

"Don't bother," Nathan says. "I like living out here. The nature and shit. It's a nice change of pace from the highways and concrete. At night, it's a different story."

"Can't sleep?"

He shakes his head. "Not for shit."

"You slept tonight."

"Only 'cause you were here." He shifts closer and closer until he ends up half on top of me. Chin on my chest, he gazes into my eyes, and his stare is so intense that for a moment, he looks like he wants to eat me. "Without you, my world's all black."

Nathan says the most outrageous things without meaning them, but this feels all too real, and I swallow against the lump forming in my throat.

"Don't say that."

"Why not?" he mutters. "It's the truth. You wanted me to open up to you, didn't you?"

"Not if it's just gonna be yet another manipulation tactic."

"I'm not trying to manipulate you. I'm trying to make you mine."

Mine how? *My friend, my boyfriend, my sex toy?* To Nathan, there's unlikely to be a difference, and what comes out of my mouth I neither planned for nor expected to say.

"If I'm yours, then you're mine."

His eyes widen, and with a sharp exhale of breath, he hisses, "Fuck." He climbs on top of me, pinning me to the bed. "Yeah, I can be yours."

I grab both his ass cheeks, kneading them as he grinds down on me. "At the very least, you're my hole. My slut."

He's hard already, and his small, desperate whimper makes my own cock twitch and swell. He gets hold of the bottle of lube on the nightstand and squeezes a dollop onto his fingers. Then he reaches behind himself, and ...

"Shit." It's my turn to hiss as he pushes his fingers inside himself. I'm rock-hard in seconds as he looks down at me, cheeks flushed, wanton need written all over his features.

He seems desperate to do it—desperate to get my cock inside him. He ruts against me, whining and gasping. Then he pulls his fingers out and grabs the base of my cock, sliding the sensitive crown along his tight, puckered hole.

"Condom," I grit out.

He shakes his head. "Want you to fuck me raw. Wanna feel your cum inside me."

"We can't. It's not ... it's not safe."

"Why, you think I'm some disease-ridden whore?"

I try to scoff, but it comes out more of a groan as the tip of my cock nudges against his opening. Given his recklessness when it comes to ... well, everything, a lack of protection would hardly be the worst of his missteps.

"For your information," he says, "I tested myself before I came here."

"And?"

"*And* I'm fine." He lines himself up and bears down.

"But I haven't ...," I say, teeth gritted, having to muster up all my self-control not to grind upward, "... gotten tested." I had it done before Lydia and I got together, but since then I've lacked both the time and the headspace. Because of ... reasons. The reasons being mostly Nathan.

"I don't care. Fuck me. Now." The words are raw in his throat, teetering on the edge between a command and a plea. He aligns our bodies, breaching himself on the head of my cock. Eyes closed, he ruts his hips, burying my cock inside him. He seems lost in another world—a perfect world of blissful pleasure. His mouth falls open, and his eyebrows pinch, the tousled locks of his hair bouncing as he moves.

"Fucking perfect," he whispers.

It's done. There's no more use in acting prim and proper, because apparently Nathan is depraved enough to override all semblance of safety, and with the next rut of his hips, he snaps the already thin thread of my sanity as well.

I grip his buttocks harder, kneading them in the back-and-forth motion. "You like my cock that much, huh?"

"Like it? I fucking love it. Love everything you do to me."

"Oh yeah?" In one swift motion, I flip him over, and he lands on his back with a huff. With my knees under his thighs and my hands on his hips, I gain a better position to really hammer into him. Slow and deep at first, making him moan. Then fast and rough, my balls slapping against his quivering ass. I want to stretch him wide open, fuck him so hard he'll always feel me.

Arm muscles straining as I pull him back and forth on my cock, I shift my hips, trying to hit his prostate.

His eyes widen as his cock twitches and dribbles with precum. "Oh god."

"Yeah, there you go."

"Wanna come," he whines, meeting my thrusts so desperately our skin slaps with obscene sounds.

"Go ahead, baby." The term of endearment comes out without warning, and why did it feel so right?

I want to see just how much his pretty little ass can take. I want to fuck him until he's a ruined, sweaty mess, until he's covered in my nail and bite marks. I want to fuck him until he's too exhausted to string two words together.

And I want to fuck him until he's mine, through and through.

But my what?

My friend? Well, we're way past that. Boyfriend? I don't know. All I know is I want him to stay, and I don't want him to suffer except by my hand.

I don't want to find him on the kitchen floor again. I need to make sure he's safe, away from this haunted, horrible house where he endured so many horrible things.

He needs someone to take care of him. He should be in my bed, in my arms, where no one can harm him and none of our pasts can come back to haunt us.

If only I can erase the last five years from my mind, I'll have what I've always wanted. When we were kids, I wanted him, and when we got older, I wanted him in a different way.

Now I have him, and nothing can make me give that up. He's mine. My hole. My slut. My baby.

A growl rumbles in my chest as I keep drilling my cock into him. "Gonna come inside you now. That's what you wanted, huh?"

"Yeah," he gasps. "Oh god, yeah ..." He wraps his hand around his straining cock and gives it a few jerks, and then he's erupting all over his stomach and chest.

I follow suit, emptying myself inside him. With a satisfied grunt, I collapse on the side of the tiny bed, crowding him against the wall.

He brings a hand to his chest, wipes up the cum there, and licks it up. Yeah, he's a slut all right.

I press a kiss to his cum-stained lips. "You shouldn't have done that."

"What?"

"Made me fuck you without a condom." I push him to lie on his side and slip my hand between his buttocks to tease his sticky, stretched hole.

He makes a sound between a snort and a moan. "Oh, please. As if you didn't wanna blow your load in me."

I feel it trickling out of him, lukewarm and thick. I catch it with my finger and push it back inside.

"You really want to do this?" He thrusts his ass back against my hand. "You really want to make me horny again?" He climbs on top of me, once again straddling my hips. "I could do this all day, you know. Give me a bump and a bottle of lube, and I'll let you fuck me until my eyes bulge out of my head."

"How about we don't do drugs—how long would you last, then?"

He snorts. "Your loss."

Soon enough I'm fully hard again, and he grabs my cock and guides it back to his hole. I groan as the sensitive tip slides past his tight rim. He tilts his head back, and I trace my fingers over his neck. Even though I barely applied any pressure, his skin is slightly bruised from last night. For someone with such a dirty mouth and sky-high emotional walls, he bruises easily on the outside.

"I'd do this for you, you know," I tell him, wrapping my hand lightly around his throat. "But we should talk about things like this beforehand. You may feel like you want it in the moment, when really it's not what's best for you."

"I don't care what's best for me."

"I know you don't, but I do."

He stops moving, and the way he looks at me sends a chill down my spine. "Do you, now?"

What the hell?

"I won't ever hurt you, Nate."

"Well," he says with a sneer. "A little too late for that." He swings his leg off me, and my cock slides out of his slippery hole. "I'm gonna go shower." He grabs a shirt from the floor, uses it to wipe the cum off his belly, and tosses it carelessly on the bed. And just like that, he's off.

"What the fuck." I groan and lean back in the bed, left with a flagging hard-on and a head full of questions.

I don't get him.

I really don't.

I spend the workday rewinding the morning in my head. When I come home, I'm exhausted in both mind and body.

It's weird—I want to drive back to his place and see him, but at the same time, I need the alone time that used to be a constant point of tension with my girlfriends.

Nathan was once exempt from my need for isolation, but not anymore.

Now he confuses and frustrates me too much. I mean, what was that cryptic shit about me not wanting what's best for him? Granted, I *did* want to kill him when he first came back to town, but recently everything has changed. And I took care of him when we were younger, didn't I? With any luck, things will ease up between us once I get him out of that creepy old house.

I catch George in the kitchen, frying up what smells like shrimp and fried rice.

"Any luck with that roommate ad?" I ask casually as I get myself a glass of water.

He shrugs. "I've vetted a few, but nothing's set in stone yet."

I decide it's better to be frank with this. George prefers honesty above all else, after all. Maybe that's why he and Nathan get along so badly.

"Nathan needs a place to stay."

He sends me a slow, calculating look. "I thought he was staying at his mom's place."

"Well, he is, but—"

"But what? That old shack not up to his standards? I thought he was used to sleeping in his car."

"Will you let me finish?"

"It depends. Are you asking what I think you're asking?" He turns from the stove to look at me, *really* look at me, eyes burrowing into me with intent, and his voice drips with near disgust as he asks, "Are you fucking him?"

"Yeah," I say with a shrug, though my heart starts pounding in my chest. I like to think I don't care what George thinks of me, but he was the one to drag me out of my depressive hole a few years back. He was there for me when no one else was, and he deserves ... I don't know what he deserves. Shit, I don't even know what I'm doing.

"He's not a good person, Daniel," he says in the tone of my father and uncle: slow and firm and commanding.

"If *he's* not a good person, what does that make your dad?"

He falters, eyes narrowing. "What?"

"Nathan told me all about Wayne's visits to Theresa. Did you know?"

"Daniel, that's ..."

"Did you know he gave her drugs too?"

His cheeks go bright red, and the vein in his temple starts to pulse. "You know you're playing right into his hands, right?"

Just then, April enters the room. "Some people are trying to study, you know. What's going on in here?"

"Daniel wants Nathan to move in with us," George says in a tone that makes it sound like I want us to finance him a trip to outer space or something.

"Oh. I thought he already had a house?"

"He's in a bad way out there," I say. "He needs me."

"Needs you to stroke his ego maybe," George says. "Fucking hell, Daniel, you're more gullible than I thought."

"His mom died, if you forgot."

"So what, didn't she beat him or something? From what I know, he hated her guts."

"All the more complicated," April says. "The death of your abuser, look it up."

George waves a dismissive hand. "That guy doesn't have the capacity for grief."

"Fuck off, that's not true," I growl.

"I'm guessing he still doesn't have a job?"

"No."

"What's his plan, then?"

"We ... haven't really talked about that."

"I heard Sidney's needs people."

"Sidney's?" I can't for the life of me picture Nathan flipping burgers and taking orders. I have a hard enough time wrapping my head around his odd jobs on the road.

"What, he's too fancy for a burger joint?" George sneers. "He doesn't have a degree, so—"

"Neither do I," I cut in.

"—it's either that, drug-dealing, or whoring, but I assume he's already tried the latter." The mocking glint in his eyes makes my blood boil.

April slaps his arm. "That's not it at all. Let's look at it like this: What sort of stuff is he good at? People? Things? Animals?"

"I don't know," I say. "But even if he'd get a job, he can't think straight when he's living in that house."

George shakes his head. "You can't keep doing this, Daniel. He's just using you and taking advantage of your kindness. That's what people like him do."

April's black-painted nails pull at a thread in her cardigan, a thoughtful smile on her lips. "I don't know. He didn't seem so bad. He was funny." She wiggles her eyebrows at me. "And cute as hell."

George scoffs. "Yeah, yeah, we all know how hot he is. That ain't even half the point, though it sure doesn't help the situation. And this is all without even mentioning what he does to Daniel."

"And what does he do to me exactly?"

George looks at me as if I'm the most gullible person in the world. "He hurt you, didn't he? He left town and changed his number like he didn't even know you. But I know you, and nothing you could have done would've warranted that."

I'm not so sure anymore. The venomous look in Nathan's eyes this morning spoke differently.

George sighs and points between the three of us. "Look. This is what he does; he drives wedges between people. He'd be rubbing his hands in delight right now if he heard our squabbling."

"Fine," I say. "Let's hear the verdict, then."

"I wouldn't mind him moving in," April says. "At least for a time."

"Well, I would mind," says George. "He's not some homeless puppy, Daniel, and we sure as hell aren't a shelter. And by the way, don't think I've forgotten how you acted at the party."

"How *I* acted?"

"You stepped in front of him and told *me* off. As if he wasn't the one who started that shit in the first place! He doesn't need your protection, Daniel."

"Apparently he does, since you fucking hit him!"

"Don't tell me he didn't deserve it. He was begging for it, in fact."

"It's not up to you to decide what he deserves," I growl.

"No? 'Cause that's *your* job?"

"Guys!" April yells over our raised voices. "Enough. Going by our house rules, we all have to agree about a new roommate. I'm sorry, Daniel. I do hope to see more of you though. You've been so *busy* lately." She winks and gives me a sly look.

"Don't count on it," George says. "Now that Nathan's back, Daniel won't pay much attention to his other friends."

Well, that went to shit.

If I can't even find a place for Nathan to live in the short term, how can I hope to make him stay in the long term?

I need something—other than sex—that will root him in the here and now. Something to connect him to this town. To me. I need to make him remember the good times we shared here. And then hopefully he'll realize it's madness to live in his childhood home.

It's a bit of a stretch, I do realize, but it's what's on my mind and keeps interrupting my attempts to practice my pencil drawing techniques. I've been so scatterbrained lately that I've neglected my art. Although I've banished it to hobby territory for now, it's still one of the things—along with physical activity—that keeps me sane and level-headed.

At least, it used to.

I give up on the drawing. Instead, I look through the set of Polaroids for the fifth or sixth time. Nathan's confident grin shines back at me, his arms around my shoulders, me smoking a joint ...

But something is missing. I shift through them all once more, and yeah—my sketch of us by the mansion at Mumphrey Hill is nowhere to be found. I look in the other drawers and under the bed. Nothing.

Did *he* take it?

I imagine him sitting on his bed in his dark, run-down room, a smile on his lips as he studies the picture in his hand.

And suddenly I know what to do.

Chapter 11

NATHAN

It's a rainy, miserable fuckup of a morning. And what makes it even more miserable? Daniel's not here.

He didn't come over yesterday, so I had to spend the night alone, and as a result I got barely two hours of sleep. My head hurts, my chest hurts, everything fucking hurts, and it's his fault.

When my phone pings, I know it's him. Who else would it be?

Come over this afternoon. I want to show you something.

My heart lifts in my chest, and my mouth curls into a smile. Just as soon, I squeeze the phone in my hand, scowling at my own reaction. I don't need to come running to him; he can come to me. Once he realizes I'm not showing up, he'll come here without a doubt.

I roll a joint out of my rapidly dwindling stash of weed and sit on the porch. Sometime this past week, the leaves have rotted off the trees, and the gusts of wind blowing through my hair are harsher and colder than before. The dreary clouds and pouring rain fit my mood just fine.

The wind lashes through the house, and the wood creaks ominously. I get what Daniel means; the place is creepy as hell. It's mine though, and the darkness here is in me too. I was born in that darkness, and it's followed me all my life.

Five years of escaping it hasn't changed a thing. I'm still that terrified boy, curled up in the corner of my room. I'm still that pissed-off teenager, plotting to kill my mom for all the shit she put me through. And the greatest irony of all? She went and pissed me off one last time, by dying before I could do the deed myself.

Jagger barks somewhere up the road. Old Ennis is probably trudging along, business as usual. He better not come around here though. I don't mind company per se, but last time we spoke ended up a disaster.

Whenever I feel like this—like a thousand ants are clawing at my insides—I would go to Moe's Den in a heartbeat, but the thought of a sweaty, hairy biker panting down my neck isn't nearly as appealing as it used to be.

Daniel must really have done a number on me. Monogamy is one thing. This obsession, this need to be close to him ... That's a whole other animal, and it should bother me more than it does. But for the most part, it feels ... good. As long as I'm with him, that is. As long as I'm nuzzling into his jaw while his strong arms close around my waist.

Alone, I'm no good at all. I feel like I'm coming apart at the seams.

The weed does a decent job of calming me down though. Some of my restless energy dissolves, and together with my head clearing up, the truth hits me like a wave.

None of how I feel is Daniel's fault; it's all mine. My fault for depending on him. My fault for letting him see me a blubbering, crying mess. My fault for living on the impossible hope that this thing between us won't fall off a cliff steep enough to shatter my bones.

If it does, I have my backup plan, of course: my grandpa's shotgun in the hallway closet. I don't know how to use it exactly, but I'll figure it out.

I flick the joint away and pull my knees to my chin, hugging my legs. This just proves it, doesn't it? I'm the same as before. I've always been shit at being alone. I need people, even though I hate needing them. Anyone used to suffice—anyone who'd give me their company and their dick, no matter how horribly they treated me.

Not anymore. Now I need Daniel. Fuck, I need him so bad.

I tap my thumbs on the steering wheel to the furious rhythm of a metal song.

I pass the local antique shop and the shabby-looking middle school I attended before my transfer to Daniel's class. Oh, and there's the grocery store where Wayne Hastings caught me red-handed.

It feels like ages since I last left my hovel. Maybe the isolation was getting to me a bit. Anyway, as soon as I see Daniel, I should be all right. I ring the bell to his house, and a black-haired girl with tattoos opens the door. It's that girl from the party. What was her name again? April.

"Oh," she says, beaming at me. "What gives me the honor?"

If I'd had less of a bad day, I wouldn't mind putting my charm on and playing the game of social niceties. But not today. Today I go straight to the point.

"Where's Daniel at?"

Her smile doesn't budge. "He's still at work. You're welcome to wait inside if you'd like."

"No, thanks." The words come out on their own. I'm not sure why. Maybe it's because April gives off the same vibe I used to get from my English teacher. They both strive to make me feel comfortable in their company—comfortable enough to make me spill my inner thoughts.

In third grade, Miss Allister sat me down in her office. Her eyes looked so warm and so patient that I almost told her everything. Only the thought of the beating I'd get if my mom ever found out kept me from it.

No one would beat me now, but the apprehension remains.

April grabs my wrist, her hand cool and soft. "Come on. I've got a pot of tea brewing."

I grimace but allow her to pull me inside. So what if she wants to ask me questions? I can simply refuse to answer, or do what I do best: lie.

———

April smiles at everything I say, laughs at my jokes, and feeds me copious amounts of snacks. This isn't so bad. It's pretty fun actually. I'd rather hang out with Daniel though. The clock on the kitchen wall is approaching four, yet he still hasn't arrived.

"I get it now," April says in between giggles. "I get why Daniel likes you so much." She sends me a thoughtful look. "He's changed since you arrived, you know."

"Changed how?"

"For one, he's smiling more. He used to spend hours alone in his room, drawing or brooding or whatnot. When he wasn't hanging out with his girlfriends, that is."

"Oh yeah? How many girlfriends are we talking?"

"You're not jealous, are you?" she teases.

Jealous isn't the right word, but the thought of Daniel with someone else ... Well, I don't like it. Not one bit.

"You shouldn't be," April says. "Daniel never cared about any of them like he cares about you."

"How do you know?" I keep my voice casual, but inside I'm aching for the answer.

"Well, he never argued for any of *them* to move in with us."

"He didn't have to do that," I mutter. "I'm fine where I am."

"He's probably just worried about you."

"What's there to worry about?"

April grows quiet for a moment and leans her cheek in her hand. "That house you live in, did you grow up there?" She says it lightly, as if she doesn't care for the answer either way, but I know better: This is all just a ruse to get my guard down. And it's working.

"Yeah. With my mom."

"Have you talked with someone about it?"

"About what?"

"About your mother."

I frown and lean back in the chair, away from her inquiring gaze. "Why would I do that?"

"She passed away. For most people, that's complicated stuff, too complicated to sort through on your own."

"I'm not on my own." *I have Daniel.*

"There are people you can talk to, you know."

"What, you mean a shrink?" I scoff. "They'll just push a bunch of pills on me. Been there, done that." When I was eight, the doctors wanted to put me on ADHD meds for my supposed attention disorder, but the pills made me even more sleepless than I already was and laced my anxiety with fits of anger I couldn't control. Besides, they were far too expensive for my mother to pay for.

"It's worth a try," April says. "I talk to a therapist myself, I could give you her number if—"

"I'm fine."

"Sure you are, but we all need someone who listens to us at times."

"Daniel listens to me."

April makes a face halfway between a grimace and a smile. "Daniel's a good guy, don't get me wrong, but he has his head in the clouds most of the time. He's more of a hands-on type than a listener. That guy doesn't see more than two feet in front of him, too wrapped up in his own world. Not like you. You like to escape yourself, am I correct?"

"I don't think ahead. I just do what feels good."

"But what feels good sometimes leads to bad things, doesn't it?"

My mouth pulls tight, and I don't feel like saying much more, so I don't. Somewhere along the way, I lost control of this conversation, and I need to get it back.

April's warm brown eyes study me for longer than I'm comfortable with, and her voice grows quiet and soft. "I get why he wants to help you so badly."

"Help me?" I smirk, hoping to throw her off guard. "All men want is a tight hole to fuck."

She huffs out a startled laugh. "Is that what you think?"

I thread my fingers behind my neck and lean back in the chair. "Well, that and fat stacks of cash."

"What about Daniel?"

"What about him?"

"He seems to want more from life. From you."

"Maybe. Maybe not." *Maybe he's just fooled himself I'm worth his time. Once he finds out what a fuckup I truly am, he'll be disgusted with himself—with me—and completely regret the effort.*

"What do you do out there anyway, at that house?" April asks.

"Nothing much." *I disintegrate piece by piece, plagued by memories of my messed-up past.*

"If you want something to do, there's an animal shelter up north. They always need staff. Doesn't pay much, but if you want to stay in town, it might be worth looking into."

I roll my eyes. "I take it Daniel's been yapping about me?"

"He doesn't say much, but when he says something, he really means it." Her eyes twinkle. "Unlike ..."

"Yeah, yeah, unlike me. What can I say? I've got a talent for running my mouth."

"I get it. George is the same."

Me? The same as George? I resist the urge to dry-heave at the idea.

"How are you able to stand that guy anyway? You're ..." I gesture wildly at her. "You're actually nice. Unlike him."

"George can be nice," April says, "if you've earned his trust. What can I say, I like a guy with steadfast principles." She leans over the table and speaks in a softer tone. "He doesn't hate you or anything, you know. He's just protective of Daniel and worried you'll hurt him."

"I don't plan to hurt him."

"I didn't say you do."

Footsteps creak on the porch outside.

"I know!" George exclaims as the door swings open. "But that's just the thing. We'll never get it under control if we don't—" He stops in his tracks as he catches sight of me. "Oh. *You're* here."

I sling my arm over the back of the chair. "Lovely to see you too."

Daniel pushes past his cousin. The sight of him in gym clothes and sweaty hair makes saliva pool in my mouth.

"You're late," I tell him. I get up from the chair and cross my arms, leaning against the table.

"Gym session. If you'd checked your phone, you would've known." His eyes flit between the three of us. "April, can you make sure these two don't kill each other while I go change?"

"Sure thing," April says.

George rounds on me. "So he doesn't even check his phone?" he says, talking to me in third person as if I'm a child. "What *does* he do?"

"Go back to your law books, Georgie."

"Fuck off," he growls.

A thrill goes through me, sizzling down to my very bones. Once I smell blood in the air, I'm hopeless to resist. Today I'm strung tight enough to snap, and given the right opportunity, I will. George's face in front of mine is an opportunity if I ever saw one.

"Why are you here, anyway?" he asks. "I don't see an invitation."

"Daniel invited me. I guess he needed a break from you."

"It's *you* he needs a break from. You were always like this—popping up where you weren't wanted. Following him around like a lost puppy."

"Why do you care so much about him anyway?" I cup my jaw in exaggerated contemplation. "It's a little creepy if you ask me. Is there something you haven't told us?"

April snorts with laughter. "Oh, honey, come on, that was pretty funny," she says when George shoots her a glare.

He turns back to me, nostrils flaring. "You should leave. Nobody wants you here. Well, Daniel might, but he sure as hell doesn't *need* you."

"Daniel needs me," I say. Right on cue, Daniel comes down the stairs, looking hot as ever in a tight blue T-shirt and ripped jeans. "You need me, right, babe?"

He gestures to the hallway. "Let's go. My car's low on gas, so we'll take yours, but I'm driving."

George whirls around. "Where are you going with *him*?"

"See?" I stick my tongue out at George as I pass him in the hallway. "Daniel loves me. He hates you."

"Now listen here, you little shit ..."

"He eats my ass too."

"We're leaving." Daniel grabs my arm and pulls me outside, but not before I get one last glance at George, who looks like he's about to explode. He's lucky Daniel's grip on me is tight like a vise. I wouldn't mind staying a bit longer and showing him exactly what it means to mess with me. But I better not.

Daniel chose me. He chose me over George. The thought is enough to put a spring in my step as I hurry to keep up with his long strides. He climbs into my car and slams the door shut. As soon as I land in the passenger seat, he turns to me.

"Would you stop acting like a three-year-old around him for one fucking day?"

"Me? What about *him*?"

"Look." He sighs. "I want you to get along with my friends, okay?"

"George is your cousin, not your friend."

"The two aren't mutually exclusive."

"They should be."

"Can you at least *try* to be civil with him?"

My lip curls. "Why?"

He starts counting on his fingers. "One: I live with him. Two: He's my friend, whether you like it or not. Three: It's a small town. You two are bound to run into each other."

"Daniel, he hit me."

"You hit him too."

I give him a sharp look. "Oh, so you think 'cause I broke his nose six years ago when he was being a jerk, he should be allowed to hit me whenever he wants?"

"You know that's not what I think, and I talked to him about it."

"And?"

"He's ... sorry."

"Sure." Arms crossed, I slump back in the seat and send him the side-eye. "Admit it—you like me like this. You like my bite."

He raises a hand and runs his thumb over my lower lip. "I like you better when you're begging for my cock."

"That so?" I reach over and slide a hand over his thigh. "How much begging are we talking?"

"Today, not so much. You owe me one."

I owe him a blow job for fucking around with George? Fine by me.

"Did you tell him about us, by the way? He seemed more pissed at me than usual."

"He figured it out." Daniel leans back, unzips his jeans, and pulls out his cock. My mouth waters at the sight. "Hurry up. The sun's setting."

"Where are you taking me anyway?"

"Mumphrey Hill."

I lean over the center console, and he pushes me down with a decisive grip on my hair. My throat tingles as I inhale his musky scent through my nose, tongue gliding down his girthy shaft.

Mumphrey Hill, huh. And what memories does he want us to pull up from that old shithole?

Chapter 12

DANIEL

My head feels suspiciously empty when I exit the car. Nathan must have sucked some of my brain matter out with that blow job. No wonder he's so proud of his dick-sucking skills; he's a fucking master and he knows it.

The decrepit, unfinished mansion of Mumphrey Hill looms up ahead. Legends say it was commissioned by some hotshot investor whose business went under before the construction finished, and the place got stuck in legal limbo. With time, it became the refuge and playground for the town's delinquents.

Delinquents like me and Nathan.

The proximity to our high school meant we could bike up here during lunch recess. We sprayed the white marble walls with graffiti. We smoked weed, listened to music, and enjoyed the view of Springvale's prime vantage point. We even lived here a whole summer when we were fourteen.

Every time I think of it, I can't help but smile. Nothing has come close to that summer so far, and maybe nothing ever will.

We spend the rest of the evening exploring the rooms. We zigzag across the pillars and the curved ceiling of what should have been a luxurious bedroom, pass the half-finished bathroom and the ruined shell of the downstairs kitchen.

Now it's all crumbled, and every inch of the walls is covered in graffiti.

Somewhere in here lives an echo of our former selves. I hoped we could find some sign of us—some remnant of our ghosts and the people we were—but there's nothing. Only cigarette butts, dirty tissues, and old, damp sleeping bags.

We end up in the backyard, on the concrete block we used to fashion as a bench. Nathan lights a joint and hands it to me. This time, I take it. Cupping my hands as I light it up feels so habitual, so right, that I wonder why I even quit in the first place.

Together we watch the sun descend below the mountains at the opposite end of town. The once first-rate view of the city is now half-concealed by vegetation, but the ancient cedar woods around Springvale's campus are the same, as is the smoke from the paper mill, the sprawling suburban houses, and the quaint city center.

My home. Our home.

"Look familiar?" My exhale drifts through the wind, merging with the brilliant orange sunset.

Nathan takes the joint from my hand with a brow raised in question.

"I had a sketch of this place," I clarify. "You stole it."

He flashes his teeth in a grin. "I did?"

"Don't deny it."

"It was a good one," he says, as if it's explanation enough. "We had a good time out here."

"Yeah. That summer ... it means a lot to me."

"Me too." He slides his hand over mine and leans his head on my shoulder. The moment feels frozen in time, like two pictures snapping into place, our past and our present selves merging into one.

"Holy shit I missed you so much," I croak, and the tightness rushing up my chest isn't just from the weed. I feel like crying and laughing all at once.

"I know, Daniel. I missed you too."

Why do I still not fully believe him? Even though five years have gone and passed, one particular wound is still too raw when pressed on. And yet I can't help but dig into it, rip the half-healed tissue apart and claw it open.

He said he cared about me when we were growing up. But if that's true, how could he have hurt me like that? Will he ever become the person he was to me back then? Do I even want him to be? By even entertaining the idea, I open myself up for destruction. For heartbreak.

What are you doing? A cruel tilt of perfect lips as I leaned in to kiss him. *What did you think—that we're some lovey-dovey couple now? Fucking is just fucking.*

My heart pounds, hard and deep. Crap. This is why I don't smoke anymore. George made me quit my daily use after I dropped out of college, and every time I've tried it since then has devolved into a panic attack.

There's a rumble behind the mansion. Engines? Motorbikes? My hypervigilant senses have me jumping off the bench and looking through the broken windows to the driveway.

At least five or six bikes and as many men are parked by the entrance.

"Nate," I hiss. "What the fuck are they doing here?"

Nathan hasn't even left the bench, still puffing on the joint. "Some stuff going on with a handover, most likely."

"A handover?"

The men dismount their bikes, and the scrawny, insect-like form of Joshua enters my view. He gives one of the bikers a packet of some kind, and he receives one in return. Drugs? Money?

The bikers leave soon after, but Joshua stays put. Why isn't he leaving?

"I know you're here," he calls. "You think I don't recognize that ugly car of yours, Antler?"

"Shit." My voice sounds too loud to my ears. I feel hot all over, almost sick. "Nate, get the fuck up."

Joshua walks across the ruined kitchen with no care in the world, and I stand to face him.

"What do you want?" I ask.

He nods toward Nathan, who's still sitting with his back turned, seemingly unbothered.

"You owe me quite a bit of cash, Antler. Or did you forget?"

"I haven't forgotten shit," Nathan says.

"'Cause if it's gonna be a problem, I've got some ways to sort it out. I hope it won't come to that though. Would hate to ruin that pretty face."

Nathan just snorts.

"Or how about you, Hastings?" Joshua asks, eyes on me. "You'd take a bullet for him, wouldn't you?"

I would. I would have when we were teenagers, and I would now.

Nathan rises slowly. He exhales a billowing cloud of smoke and puts out the joint with his boot. Without a word, he glowers at Joshua as if trying to burn a hole in him with sheer will of mind.

"We'll bring you the money," I say. "Just tell us when and where."

Joshua shrugs his thin shoulders. "I'm having a party at my place next Friday. Bring it then."

"Four grand, was it?"

"Four and a half. For interest."

"Fine," I say, though I don't know if it is. My own bank account echoes emptily, and about Nathan's finances I frankly have no clue. He told me he's got the money, but he might as well be as poor as me. Or he's got a hundred grand hidden somewhere in the Arizona desert for all I know. "We'll be there."

"You better," Joshua says and saunters off.

I spin to Nathan. "What the hell was that?"

"What?" he mutters. He kicks an empty beer can out of the way, walks to the next in line, and does it again.

"We're not kids anymore, Nate, and these people aren't joking around. I won't let you ruin your life and your future."

In the middle of a kick, he stops and looks up at me. "Future? What future? What about you—you gonna work as a janitor forever? I thought you were going to be an artist."

"Yeah well, sometimes shit doesn't work out. But what's the alternative, huh? Deal dope with Joshua and end up in prison, or worse?"

"At least in prison, I wouldn't have you nagging me to death."

"Fuck!" I turn my back on him, clenching my fists so hard my arms shake. So this is how it's gonna be? I might have tolerated his erratic bullshit back when we were younger, but not anymore. I'm tired of this. I'm tired of *him*.

"Daniel." His voice is soft now, concerned, as if he's realized he went too far. "Daniel," he repeats and puts a hand on my trembling shoulder. "Daniel, I'm sorry."

The buzzing in my ears drowns out everything except the rare set of words only I have the privilege to hear. The vulnerability offered to no one but me. Because I've never heard Nathan apologize to anyone else; it just doesn't happen. And the tone of his voice? That careful, soft, worried one? A fucking unicorn in the context of all the other shit he says.

"We'll go together, all right?" he says. "I'll get it done."

"You will?"

"Yeah. But could you …" His voice breaks, and he seems to force out the next sentence. "Could you come stay with me for a while? I can't sleep when you're not around, and I don't … I don't want to be alone out there."

His voice is shaking, and he sounds so pitiful I have to turn to look at him. He's got his arms wrapped around himself, and his head hangs on his chest. He looks younger than I've ever seen him. Dejected. Worried. Regretful.

Still, I can't help but wonder if he's faking all this. Is it all just a trick to get my guard down? It wouldn't be the first time he tried something similar.

But no … Manipulative tendencies aside, Nathan isn't this good of an actor, and he wouldn't ask such a thing of me if he didn't mean it.

My moment of consideration is mostly for show. He has to sweat a bit and realize he can't get away with things so easily. I can't leave him hanging for very long though; can't stand to have him look at me with those dejected puppy eyes.

"Okay, let's make a deal: You pay Joshua what you owe, and I'll come stay with you."

He won't move into my house anytime soon, so staying at Wayward Road might be the best option for now. At least there I can keep an eye on him. I want to know when he's hurting, and I want to make him not hurt anymore. I want to cook him dinner every night. I want to wake up every morning to his sleepy, soft smile.

His jaw clenches in consideration for a moment before he nods. "Yeah. Yeah, that's fine. So you'll come home with me?" he asks, hope written all over his features.

"Yeah. I'll come home with you."

That night, I lie awake and listen to his breathing. I pray he has a dreamless sleep, without any nightmares or vicious thoughts.

Instead, I'm the one who dreams.

I'm standing in the middle of a dark void. Nathan is there, in the distance with his back turned. I run to him, but as soon as my body crashes into his, he evaporates from my embrace like thin smoke. I turn around and see his body take shape anew. I embrace him again, and again he disappears.

It continues in loops, over and over, until one time, I cannot find him again. I roam the dark void for hours, for days. But he's gone. He's left me again.

I'm alone.

I wake up with a jolt. My heart is racing, and cold sweat seeps through my skin. I shift to Nathan's side and clutch him close. He makes a soft sound in his sleep and presses against me.

My heartbeat slows, but the feeling of helplessness in my chest won't abide. I lie awake for a long time, listening to the creaks of the wind rushing through the house.

I refuse to let anything happen to him. He's mine now, and I won't let him go. But what if I can't stop him slipping away from me? What if one day, he's just gone without a word?

I can't go through that again. I just can't.

I grip him closer, inhaling the smell of his hair. He sighs in his sleep and nuzzles into my neck.

I hold no illusions I can pin him down like I pinned him with my body last night. Any day now, something can go wrong, and I'll be hopeless to stop him from turning his back on me again.

Chapter 13

NATHAN

Daniel crosses his arms, leaning against the bathroom doorway. "I told you; I won't choke you again until we have a safe word."

I pop the mascara wand back into its tube. "And I've told *you* just to pick one."

"Even if we had one, would you use it?" The insistence in his voice, that moralizing, highbrow challenge in his eyes ... He doesn't get it.

I want to feel like I'm sinking into someone else's mercy. I want to lose control and let go of myself, let go of everything. I've tried explaining this to him about a hundred times in the past two weeks.

If I can just say a word or make a gesture and be in control again in the blink of an eye, it defeats the purpose ... But maybe that's just my nonexistent sense of self-preservation talking.

"I trust you. And I trust you not to hurt me for real."

He shakes his head. "But I don't trust *you*, how about that?"

I scowl into the mirror, tracing my eyes with a thin layer of eyeliner. He'll come around soon enough. Choking is off the menu, but he holds no qualms about spanking my ass until it's red like a traffic sign.

For the past two weeks, we've fucked like rabbits. In every constellation imaginable, in every room of the house. I pick him up from work, we get something to eat, and then we spend the rest of the evening exploring each other's bodies. I've made a game of how quickly I can get him to come, and he's made a game of how quickly he can get me to beg for his dick. We've even set timers and everything. Needless to say, he always wins the latter.

Our newfound routine has also meant Friday came along sooner than I wanted or expected, and Friday means Joshua and his sleazy, drugged-up party.

Daniel nods at me. "Do you really have to dress like that?"

"Why? Worried I'll get unwanted attention?"

He joins me by the mirror, lines up against my back, and growls into my ear, "Yeah, that too. But mostly because I'll have trouble keeping my hands off you."

True to his words, his hands encircle my exposed midriff. The outlines of my nipples peek through the sheer material of my top, and my sleek leather pants are so tight I have trouble moving. Delicate silver feathers dangle from my earlobes, and the makeup further enhances the look: coal-black eyeliner and a trace of pink lip gloss.

"We could give them a show," I say with a grin. "These parties go pretty wild, you know. I walked in on a three-way once."

Daniel shakes his head, nose buried in the crook of my neck. His arms encase my body, and our pose emphasizes how he's taller than me, bigger than me, stronger than me. His fingers travel further up my front, slither into my top, and twist both my nipples. I lean back against him, and a groan escapes my mouth as his lips press against the line of my throat. He rolls his hips, letting me feel his swelling cock. His movements nudge the butt plug I've got secretly pushed up my ass.

"No," he says. "They don't deserve to see you like I do."

"And George says I'm the possessive one," I say with a smirk that quickly falls with another grinding motion against my ass. "How late are we?"

"Pretty late. But before we leave, can you promise me something?"

"Yeah, whatever." With my cock throbbing and the plug nudging my prostate, he can't expect me to think straight.

"Promise me you'll be careful."

"Careful how?"

"We're going to this party for one reason only. There's no need to stay longer than we have to and no need to make this a bigger problem than it is."

"Why would I cause a problem?"

He meets my gaze in the mirror, giving me a pointed look.

I roll my eyes. "You're always so fucking paranoid. Simmer down; it'll be fine. Fun, even."

"We'll see about that. You've got the money, right?"

"Yeah."

"Show me."

"Fine." I pinch the rolled-up hundred-dollar bills out of my pocket.

"I'm surprised they fit in there," he says with a smirk, sliding his hands up and down my sides. He noses into my neck. Pinches my hips. When he slots his crotch to my ass, I gasp as his movement nudges the plug deeper inside me.

"How's that ass healing up?" he asks.

"See for yourself."

He unzips me, and since I'm going commando, all the fabric he has to pull down is my pants.

"Red?" I ask.

He strokes my sore ass cheeks with his callused palms and reaches the handle of the plug that sticks out of my body. "Oh, baby," he grunts. "What's this?"

Baby? My mouth wants to smile, but I turn it forcefully into a pout. "It was supposed to be a surprise. For when we get home." I gasp as he pulls at the plug, making the flared end push against my sensitive rim.

"You wanted to be all stretched and ready for me?"

"Yeah, but ... Fuck, we're late already," I say, but my protest gets lost in the breathiness of my voice.

"Come on." His gaze is fixed to where he's fucking the plug in and out of me. He seems mesmerized by it. Every time the thickest part passes, I can't help but moan. It's my biggest plug, yet it still isn't as thick as his cock. He pauses the plug at the widest part and traces my stretched rim with a finger. "Tennyson's waited five years for that money. I think he can wait a little longer."

"Don't blame me when he and his biker friends chop us into little pieces and throw us into Blackwater Lake."

"It's worth the risk, don't you think?"

To me it's worth the risk, sure, but I didn't think the same goes for Daniel. I'm not sure how serious he is though. As for me, I'm deadly serious; I'd die to get fucked, but I wouldn't want him to go down with me. Or would I? I snort out a laugh, and the porcelain is cool against my hands as I bend toward the sink.

Daniel pulls the plug out and immediately replaces it with two fingers. He scissors them inside me, stretching my lubed-up hole.

I whimper at the sudden, demanding pleasure. "Oh fuck ..."

"Yeah, you're ready, all right. Back up a bit. Spread those cheeks like I know you like to do." He grabs the lube I keep in the bathroom for douching purposes and slicks himself up. Without much preamble, he aligns our bodies and pushes inside me.

I groan at the slight burn. "You got over your condom policy real fast."

He slides his hand into my hair and grips it sharply. "Look into the mirror. See what you look like when you're getting fucked."

I already know what I look like when I'm getting fucked. In San Francisco, I hooked up with a rich guy with a ceiling mirror above his bed, and I stared up at myself while he pounded me all night long in a meth-infused frenzy.

I do what Daniel says anyway and face my reflection. It's distorted from the diagonal crack running in the middle of the mirror, courtesy of one of my mom's many drunken outbursts.

Daniel maneuvers my knee to the edge of the sink, and the new angle allows him to hit my prostate with ruthless precision. He knows I'll go damn near delirious from this pretty quickly. I'll let him do anything to me, make me say anything ...

It's insane how fast he's adjusted to the way I need to get fucked. Although I'd prefer for him to hurt me more, to degrade me more, he makes up for it with how he swivels his hips and buries himself to the hilt, his possessive grip on my body, and the filthy things he growls into my ear.

But he doesn't fuck me like he hates me, and that's a bit of a problem. Instead of making me hate him, he makes me go soft with want, and instead of letting me give him orders, he makes me want to obey his every command.

Not that I care that much with his cock buried in my ass and his hand wrapped around my aching dick, but every time after he's wrenched the cum from my body and his own release seeps out of my ass, I feel weird.

Like I've given too much of myself away.

Like I've exposed a part of myself that's not meant to be exposed.

Like he's turned me inside out and exposed my quivering, raw insides.

And that's not a good feeling.

It's like cutting your chest open and putting your heart on offer for him to take and examine in his hand.

But Daniel won't treat it badly—he won't pluck it out of my chest and drag it through the dirt ... Right?

He buries his face in the crook of my neck as he pounds into me, and my stiff cock bobs between my legs with every thrust.

"I'm gonna plug you back up when we're done," he grunts, "so you can walk around that party with my cum still inside you. I want you to wear this too." He kisses down my throat and sucks my skin into his mouth, biting and sucking slowly, tongue flicking out to taste my sweat. "Those people should know who you belong to."

All the while, he keeps pounding me, his balls slapping against my thighs. He pulls out and slams back inside, and with a harsh grip on my hair, he urges my head to the side and covers my lips with his. I moan into his mouth.

God, I love this ...

I love him.

Wait ...

No. No, no, no ...

My eyes are wide as saucers as I stare into the mirror, and my erection wanes. Luckily Daniel doesn't seem to notice. He picks up the pace and squeezes my cock in his hand, and soon enough I'm able to relax again. When his teeth graze my skin, I shoot into his hand and all over the sink. Easy cleanup, I think distantly as the orgasm pulses through me. He follows soon after, emptying himself inside. With one swift motion, he pulls out and slides the butt plug back into my now looser hole, keeping his cum inside me.

As he pulls my pants back up, an unbidden thought creeps back into my mind. That stuff about ... about loving him.

It didn't mean anything. It was just my dick talking. I was about to come, and you think the weirdest, most fucked-up shit when you're about to come. Yeah, that's it for sure.

But the uneasy, out-of-control feeling stays, and the whole time we get ready to leave, I can barely meet his eyes.

The feeling lingers even half an hour later when we exit the car.

My veins burn with adrenaline. I feel restless and antsy, as if I've already spent six hours snorting cocaine. Some coke isn't a half-bad idea; it might help with my nerves.

Even the butt plug doesn't seem as fun of an idea as it once did. I feel it with every movement, and each time it nudges my prostate, my cock jumps in my pants. In different circumstances, being half-hard for the remainder of the night would be fun.

Music and voices boom through the thin walls of Joshua's house. Inside, there will be people I haven't seen in years. Old classmates, old enemies. People who teased and tormented me, whether for my poverty, my faggotry, or my ever-running foul mouth. Little did they know I was already used to dealing with far worse than school bullies.

One day in fifth grade, I had enough of their bullshit. I socked a kid right in the mouth and knocked half his teeth out. They ended up transferring me to Daniel's school for it. If I hadn't hit that kid, I might have never met Daniel, and then where would I have ended up? Nowhere good, that's for sure. Best decision I ever made.

Bikes and cars litter the overgrown lawn, and a Rottweiler tied to a hook in the wall is barking like mad. A bouncer stands by the entrance:

a Wolverine-looking dude who seems vaguely familiar, with a leather vest and dark sideburns.

I make a beeline toward the dog.

"Hey," the bouncer says warningly, "stay away from him, he's a beast."

I kneel and reach out a hand to the dog, fingers folded into my palm in case he lunges for a bite. He doesn't. When I come within reach, his shoulders slump, and his tail starts a tentative wag.

"You look scary, but you're just scared, aren't you?" I scratch behind his ear and take his face in my hands, rubbing him up and down his sides. "All those noises and people freak you out, huh? It's okay."

"Nate," Daniel calls. "Let's go."

"Sorry, buddy," I tell the dog. There's nothing I can do for him. I ignore the uncomfortable feeling it leaves me with and march toward the entrance with Daniel beside me.

The bouncer stops us with an outstretched hand. "Not so fast." His gaze roams over me, from my slutty outfit up to my face, and his eyes widen in recognition.

Oh. It's that biker from Moe's—the one I tried to hook up with before Daniel cockblocked us. Feels like ages have passed since then, but I suppose it hasn't been that long.

The biker shoots Daniel a glare, and I don't blame him. For this man, Daniel will forever be remembered as the guy who robbed him of a fuck. I can't help but wonder what would've happened if I'd gone with him instead. Well, it's not that hard to figure out. After I'd used him up, I would've fucked my way through town, accepting anyone who would have me. After that, I'm not so sure, but one thing I do know: I wouldn't have bothered to be here, paying off my debt. Hell, I might not have been *anywhere*.

I take Daniel's hand and look up into the biker's face with a challenge in my eyes. "Gonna let us in or what? Joshua's expecting us."

The biker scowls, but he steps aside and opens the door.

We're in. The living room is huge and sprawling. Music blares from low-quality speakers, and dozens of people are dancing, while others sit on sunken couches, snorting lines of cocaine.

I start moving toward the couches. "I wanna try some of that."

Daniel grabs my shoulder. "No, you don't." He pulls me close, his breath hot against my ear. "Keep walking." His possessive hand on my lower back as he leads me through the crowd should annoy me, but the opposite is true; it turns me the fuck on.

"Let's at least get a beer." I fish one up from an ice-filled barrel and flick it open. Daniel accepts, and I get one of my own. I chug it down while feeling people's stares at us.

Their eyes are judging, attracted, disgusted, intrigued. Women and men alike. A few guys with girlfriends stop and gawk at me. I give them a wink, but as soon as I do, I feel weird.

Long ago, I lost count of how many men I've slept with. Likewise, I've lost count of how many of them had girlfriends or wives. I know exactly what to say and how to act to get a guy's attention—even guys who claim they are straight. Funnily enough, Daniel's the one I've had to fight for the most to get into bed. Maybe that's why I can look at these men and not feel a single stir in my pants at the thought of sleeping with them. As I wade through the crowd with Daniel by my side, all I want is him. All I need is him.

I sling my arms around his neck. "Come on, dance with me."

"Let's find Joshua first, then I'll dance with you."

Way to ruin my mood, but I suppose he's right. I lead us into a second, smaller room where the music isn't quite as loud. Joshua sits on a couch with a group of his asshole friends: bikers, like the bouncer, but these are older, with hard-set, grim expressions and beards reaching down to their chests.

Joshua stands. "Look who decided to show up." He turns around the room with his hands splayed wide in a cocky gesture. "You like what I've done with the place?"

I roll my eyes. Dude's playing kingpin, but he's really just a cog in the wheel—a small player in a tiny pond. He wouldn't stand a chance in a bigger town.

"You mean how it's even more of a dump than it was? Yeah, sure. Real cute."

I feel Daniel tense up next to me. *Don't worry, babe*, I want to tell him. *I've got this.*

Back when we were small-time dealers ourselves, Daniel knew better than to get himself involved with Joshua. I didn't plan on it either, but after Daniel and I had our first falling-out after that game of spin the bottle ... Well, I suppose I flipped out a little bit. I started hanging out here with all sorts of sleazy people. Did shit I'm not proud of. At least the money I made came in handy later on.

"Well, what are you waiting for?" Joshua says. "Chop, chop. Five years is long enough, don't you think?"

My fingers clench and unclench. Part of me wants to offer him a different deal. A deal that involves me working for him. I had it all planned out in the back of my head—how I'd make my choice if I got the right vibes for it.

But now ... I glance at Daniel, and the urgency in his eyes makes me wince. Much like how I won't hit George because it would piss off Daniel, I won't entangle myself with Joshua again because Daniel would disapprove.

Gee, look at me being all righteous and shit. Does Daniel even know how fucking *special* he is? No one in the world can make me go against my own interests like this. No one but Daniel. Anything for him.

I squeeze my hand into my back pocket and fish up the tightly packed roll of bills.

Joshua's hollow-set eyes light up when I pack them into his palm. "See, that wasn't so hard, was it? I started thinking you were gonna dupe me again."

"Dupe you how?" I ask in an innocent tone, already bored of the situation.

Joshua shrugs as he counts the money. "I don't know. Disappear again. Ride off into the sunset with your boy toy Hastings."

Daniel crosses his arms. "Are we done here?"

Joshua gives me a look, not quite a smile. "Now that the nasty business is out of the way, why don't you guys stay for a bit?"

"Here?" I glance around the room. My eyes fix on the sunken leather couch, where a girl is snorting coke off an ancient-looking porn mag. She looks barely legal. Beside her sits one of the bikers, maybe even the president. A gun glimmers on the table in front of him. "No, thanks."

"Well, if you ever wanna party, you know where to go," Joshua says. "Or if you're just looking to make some friends."

I know exactly what he means by "friends." Can see it all play out like a movie in my mind. Instead of the girl, it's me on that couch, drunk and high out of my mind, kneeling between someone's legs, sucking dick for another fix. If Daniel hadn't been part of my life, that's probably where I would've ended up.

Bleak, but I've been through worse.

Daniel puts a hand on the small of my back. "We're not interested."

Joshua walks up to me, brushes a strand of hair from my neck, and smirks as he reveals my hickey.

"Don't touch him," Daniel growls.

Joshua backs away. "Do you know yet?"

"Know what?"

Joshua nods to me. "About the skeletons he's hiding in the closet."

A chill runs down my spine.

"Would explain a lot, wouldn't it?" Joshua continues. "Who knows what went on out there?"

Daniel steps in front of me, fists clenched. "What are you saying?"

I'd find the edge to his voice hot as fuck if my heart weren't pounding so damn hard. Joshua doesn't know … does he? No, there's no way, but he'll give Daniel ideas, and that's bad enough.

"Daniel, let's go," I say, grabbing his arm.

Joshua's ugly laugh echoes behind us. "Don't say I didn't warn you."

As we pass the hallway and into the main room, Daniel hisses into my ear, "What was that about?"

"What?" My pulse is still through the roof, but I work to keep my voice steady and my face a mask of arrogance.

"That stuff he said. About skeletons or whatever."

I swallow against the knot in my throat. The noises from the party are suddenly overwhelming. "You've heard about the rumors, right? That my grandpa is also my pa."

"Is that what he meant?"

"Meth heads, man," I say with a stiff shrug. "Be spinning all sorts of tales. Don't read into it too much."

"Is it true?"

"Come on, I thought I told you. Grandpa used to slap my mom around, sure, but he never did anything like that. She got knocked up in LA."

"How can you be sure?"

"Do the math, dude. She ran away at sixteen and was gone for over a year before she showed back up on his doorstep." When Daniel stays silent, I scowl and add, "What, you don't believe me? Ask Ennis. He even helped deliver me onto that rotten-ass floor. I'm not a fucking incest baby, Daniel. Thanks a lot for thinking I am."

"I didn't. I'm just trying to ..." He sighs. "I'm sorry."

"Yeah, you better be. Hope you're planning to fuck my brains out when we get home."

"I thought you wanted to dance."

We pass the dance floor, where sweaty bodies move to the offbeat techno. Ten minutes ago I would've been stoked to join them.

"Nah, this place sucks. Let's go home." I move toward the exit, but Daniel doesn't budge.

He's got his eyes on a mousy-haired girl who's staring straight at him. "Lydia."

"Daniel. How've you been?" She's got a heavy-lidded, dazed look to her eyes. Drunk? Or high?

I slide my arm around Daniel's waist from behind and peer at her. "Who's this?"

"Daniel hasn't told you about me?"

"Obviously not."

"A month ago, Daniel and I were dating. But I see his preferences have changed."

I give her a once-over. "Yeah. For the better too."

She bristles, hands on her hips. "And who are you if I may ask?"

"Uh, this is Nathan." Daniel tries to disentangle himself from my hold, but I cling to him like a baby koala. "We—"

"We go way back," I cut in. "So back off; he's mine."

Lydia stares at Daniel with an *are you serious?* expression before she says, "Well, good luck with him," and disappears into the crowd.

Daniel grabs my arm and wrenches me off him. "That was necessary as fuck. What am I going to do about you?"

"You could always try fucking me into submission," I say sweetly.

"Already tried it."

"Try harder."

He glares at me, and I smirk at him. This is all just a part of the game. He fucks me best when he's annoyed with me—pins me to the bed and takes me without mercy. My ass clenches around the plug at the thought, and my cock pulses in my pants.

We move toward the exit. At the other end of the room, Lydia is talking to a tattooed man with a bald head and heavy-lidded eyes.

Eric Fletcher.

Oh no ... Not him. Not here.

I grab Daniel's arm, but he's already on the prowl. Eric watches us approach, a dark smile on his lips.

I haven't seen him since ... Since that night.

I drank from a cup he handed me, and the next thing I knew, I landed on a bed with hands holding me down and a body on top of mine. A door slammed open, followed by the dull, fleshy sound of a fist hitting a jaw. Eric and Tyler ran off, and someone else walked toward me ...

I was gone, on autopilot, unknowing and unfeeling, but I did know this: Me naked in a bed with a guy equaled sex. That's all my mind could compute.

The morning after, when I realized what had happened, I panicked. It wasn't supposed to be like this. Daniel was meant to be different; he was meant to be safe. But he wasn't, and nothing would ever be safe again ...

"Don't!" I yell in his ear over the music. "Let's just leave." But he doesn't hear me, or he doesn't care, and soon we're in front of Eric and his friends.

"So it's true," Eric says, leaning against the wall with his arms crossed. "Joshua told me you were back in town."

Daniel jerks his head toward Lydia. "What the hell are you doing with her?"

"Oh, we're just hanging out. Already got her hooked on dope, the little slut. She was so easy, I almost feel sorry for her. But whores should be treated like whores. You'd know all about that, though, wouldn't you, Hastings?"

"What?" Daniel grits out.

Eric smirks and points a finger at me. "It's plain for everyone here to see that he's your whore."

"He's not my whore."

"No, I suppose he's not *yours* per se—he'll fuck anyone who'll have him."

"He wouldn't have *you*."

Right ... Daniel thinks Eric and Tyler roofied me and pulled me into that bedroom because I'd rejected them, but that's not it. No—a week earlier, I'd tricked them both out of a hundred bucks, and they figured a brutal ass-fucking was a fitting punishment for a faggot like me.

It made sense that they wanted me pliant for the deed; I can really fuck shit up if I want to. Little did they know, I would've gotten off on their punishment if they'd just given me a chance to agree to it. In the end, I suppose it was more about their need to dominate me. They didn't want me to enjoy it; they wanted me to suffer.

Eric uncrosses his arms and takes a step closer. "No, but you took your liberties with him, didn't you, Hastings?"

I tug on Daniel's shirt, and in a voice so thin I can barely hear myself over the music, I say, "I wanna go home."

"Yeah," says Eric, "listen to your whore."

"Fuck you," Daniel snarls and grabs my hand, and we wade through the crowd.

"You run, Hastings," Eric yells behind us. "You were always a little bitch. Fitting, isn't it? A bitch and a whore." I hear the snickers of his friends as we squeeze into the hallway and exit through the front door.

Daniel spins to me. "What's going on with you? You've been off ever since we talked to Joshua."

I sneer at him, chest clenching tight with an aggressive anxiety I can't help but show. "Well, I did just flush four grand down the toilet, and then we ran into your little girlfriend—"

"Ex-girlfriend."

"—and then you decided to have a little chitchat with a guy who fucking roofied me, maybe that's why."

"Eric deserves worse than a talking-to."

"I don't want you to get killed."

"What, you don't think I can take him?"

I frown and shake my head. "That guy's dangerous, Daniel. He used to carry knives to school and shit. Fuck, just please believe me, okay? And take me home. If you've forgotten, I've got a plug up my ass, and I've been half-hard ever since we got here."

"Okay. I'm sorry."

"Yeah, you better be," I mutter.

After he's taken me home, he proceeds to eat me out for damn near an hour, but something feels off between us. I can't put my finger on it. I find his face in the darkness and try to convert my kisses into words.

Please don't read any more into what Joshua said.

Don't investigate. Don't look into it.

Believe me. Please believe me.

Chapter 14

DANIEL

I'M JUST GOING TO check. It's probably stupid. This creepy-ass house is playing tricks on me.

All night long, Joshua's words circled back into my head.

Do you know about the skeletons he's hiding in the closet?

With the risk of being too literal, there is only one closet in Nathan's house: the old cabinet in his mom's room.

Nathan is still sleeping soundly in bed. He doesn't even have to know.

The hinges creak when I pull the doors open by their intricate, carved metal handles.

Inside, there are shelf upon shelf of old clothes and linen, and drawers full of sex toys and lingerie. On the highest shelf lies an assortment of paperwork and a small woven box. For some reason, my eyes are drawn to it, and I pull it out.

Beneath a layer of soft, crumpled paper is a photograph. A photograph of a young boy, naked on a bed. His face, scrunched up in pain, is half-hidden from the camera. He's younger than I've ever seen him, but those vivid green eyes, the straight slope of his nose, the narrow jaw …

There's no doubt. It's him.

There are dozens of them. Dozens of photos. In most, he can't be older than eight or nine. On some, there's a hand—an adult's hand, large and hairy. Oh god. He ...

The floor melts under my feet, and my stomach plunges with it.

"Daniel?" The bedsheets rustle as Nathan sits up. "What are you doing?"

"Nathan," I say, hands shaking, pulse drumming in my ears. "What the hell is this?"

His gaze lands on the box in my hands, and his eyes widen and fill with dread. For once at a loss for words, he just stares at me.

I shove the pictures back into the box. Once the initial shock has settled, my chest fills with a wild-eyed rage the likes of which I haven't felt since I barged into Eric and Tyler undressing Nathan at the grad party.

I clench my fists by my sides, and my voice comes out snarled and gritted, as if I'm trying to pass a poison. "Who did this to you?"

Nathan pulls his knees into his chest and wraps his arms around his legs, face ghostly pale.

I sit down next to him. "This is ..." I don't know what to say. Horrible? Disgusting? No word can properly describe it. "This was all before we met?" I won't be able to live with myself if this was going on while we knew each other. My guilt over not saving him from his mother is painful enough. "I thought it was Theresa who ..."

"Was a whore?" Nathan snaps. "She was. She sold herself to the local men in town, to truckers and to random passersby. To your uncle too."

"I know that. But what does it have to do with this?"

He shrugs, refusing to meet my eyes. "Let's just say some of her clients caught an interest in me too."

A cold chill runs down my spine. "You were just a little kid."

"Yes, Daniel, and that was kind of the point for them, wasn't it?"

"How often did this happen?"

"I dunno. My memory's a little hazy from that time."

"Why didn't you tell me?"

He looks up, face oddly resigned, eyes hard and narrow. No trace remains of the pale, scared kid from a few moments ago.

"Why would I? I hardly ever think about it myself. Why would I rehash that shit with you?"

"Did she know?"

He snorts out a joyless laugh. "What do you think? She orchestrated it. One of her boyfriends snapped those pictures. She was pissed off that some of her tricks were more interested in me than in her, but whatever. I assume they paid her money for it; I don't know for sure. Back then, she used to lock me up in my room a lot. It happened in here too though," he adds, eyes dark and mouth a hard line.

It happened ...

A wave of nausea rises up my throat. "Where is he now? That man?" I want to strangle everyone who's ever laid a hand on him. Theresa's fucking lucky she's six feet under.

"Long gone. Besides, he wasn't the only one."

"Tell me about them," I growl. "All of them."

"What's the point, Daniel? That shit doesn't matter anymore. None of it does."

"Don't you get it? These people need to pay for what they did to you." How can I ever find rest until they have?

Nathan just glares at me, eyes so dark they're almost black.

I have to ask. Even though the answer might shred me up inside, I have to.

"Is this why you act the way you do? With sex? Is that what this is about?" I point between us. "You and me."

"No," he says, shaking his head. "Maybe it was like that with others, but ... not with you."

"You can't pretend it doesn't affect you. Fuck, of course it still affects you. It's what living here is about, isn't it? You're stuck there, with them. You're stuck remembering it." I rake a hand through my hair. I feel like screaming, but the shock is still layered like cloying dust in my lungs. "I won't be like them, Nathan. I refuse to be one of your abusers."

His gaze cuts up to me, eyes blazing. "Oh yeah? What if you already are?"

My stomach does a flip. What the hell?

"The grad party," he clarifies. "You fought off Eric and Tyler, yeah, but then you made sure I got fucked regardless. Maybe I didn't need that from you. Maybe I wanted one fucking aspect of my life to remain pure and untainted! But no, couldn't help yourself, could you?"

"You kissed me," I whisper. "You wanted it. You told me you wanted it." I remember his arms stretching out for me, his heady voice in my ear. His lips against my neck. *Go ahead, do it. I want you to.*

"I was fucked up on vodka and whatever drug they slipped me. I barely remember shit from that night, but I sure remember you not hesitating one second to fuck me."

"Then why ... why did you ..."

"Come see you? I dunno," he says with a shrug. "I needed someone to fuck while I was here, and since you'd already shown an interest, I figured why not? Might as well be you."

"So it could have been just anyone? Anyone can fuck you and hurt you the way you want?"

I'm not special to him. I'm not special to anyone.

George has April. Mom has Jessie. I thought I had Nathan, but apparently, that ideal is further from the truth than I thought.

Nathan mumbles something that sounds like, "No, not anyone," but I'm too far gone to acknowledge his words. Something dark has dredged up from the depths of me, and there are no longer any lies he can spin for me—no manipulations he can use to reel me back in.

I can't even start to process what he told me about the grad party. It's all a jumbled, twisted mess in my head—a truth way uglier than I'm willing to accept—and I have to get away. I have to get away from him, for my sake as well as his.

"You know what?" I grit out. "I tried to give this a chance. But it's clearly not fucking working."

"You think I love this shithole town so much? You think I won't leave?"

"Maybe it's for the best. Maybe it's for the best that you do leave."

For a split second, there's stark pain in his eyes he cannot hide, but just as soon, his face morphs into an expression of fury.

"Fine!" he snaps. "But if you go now, don't bother coming back. I won't be here waiting for you."

I don't know how I make it out of the house. One second, I'm there, in the bedroom where Nathan endured so many horrors and where we shared so many precious moments together—moments that now turn sour in my mouth. The next second, I'm storming down the yard, eyes so blurry with tears I can barely see.

Damn him. Damn him! Why did he even come back? Why did he come back to *me*? Before he showed up, I was doing fine. At least I was somewhat stable, and not upended by all this goddamned frustration he awakes in me. At least I wasn't in the pain I'm in now.

I needed someone to fuck while I was here. Might as well be you.

How could I have been so fucking stupid? I wanted, so badly, to believe that what we have is more than sex, but clearly Nathan isn't capable of any real connection. Clearly he's not capable of … of loving me. Considering what he's been through, I shouldn't blame him for it, but that doesn't take away my pain.

I shove myself into the driver's seat, wipe the furious tears from my face, and start the car.

Chapter 15

NATHAN

I WAKE UP TO the familiar hit-by-a-truck feeling of a wicked hangover. I groan and roll over, but I'm not in my mother's bed; I'm in my own tiny one, and as a result, I slide off the mattress and into thin air. The pathetic thud of my limbs hitting the floor echoes through the emptiness of the house.

Right. Empty.

Daniel's gone.

He left me.

As soon as my thoughts start spinning, the pain I've done my damnedest to avoid comes rushing back. I groan and roll onto my stomach, pressing my aching forehead to the floor.

Of course Daniel had to go snooping. I should've known. It was only a matter of time before his savior complex got the better of him and, in turn, only a matter of time before he found out the true extent of how fucked up I am.

I didn't know where my mom stashed those photos, but I had my suspicions about her bedroom. Most of the pics no doubt ended up on the dark web, but for some fucked-up reason, she saved some physical copies. Why? Hell if I know.

When the time came, she and her boyfriend would give me some pills that made me sleepy. Otherwise, I would've put up a good fight. One time when I was seven or eight, I pissed them off so bad I had to flee into the woods and live there for days, in fear they'd kill me if I went back.

As the years went on, I grew older, stronger, and more defiant. Mom realized I wouldn't put up with her bullshit any longer, and as her beauty faded and her clients dwindled, her alcohol consumption shot through the roof.

Her stash came in handy last night. Half a bottle of Jack took the edge off my grief yesterday, but now it's coming back in a rage, worse than ever. Maybe I should drink the rest of the bottle to keep it at bay. Maybe I should become a drunk like her.

But that's a temporary solution. Sooner or later, I'll be sober and miserable again.

I need something permanent.

I try to move, but my head spins so bad I feel sick, and my limbs feel like I'm crawling through mud. Why should I get up anyway? Why should I get up, ever, if not to fetch my grandpa's shotgun and put an end to my misery for good?

That's a permanent solution if I've ever known one. But I'm not one to commit to permanence; I flit this way and that, like an unrestful moth in search of a light to burn me. Daniel kept me grounded for a while, sure, but it's no surprise that I can never hold on to anything good in my life.

I let out a pitiful whine. I'm such an idiot. I deserve to be out here, alone. I deserve to wallow in this house where I endured so much pain. With Daniel, things could've been different. Things *were* different with his help. The darkness in him merged with the darkness in me and became something else—something brighter. Just like when we were kids. In the years I was away from him, shit wasn't so good, but because of him—because of us—it was starting to get better.

I should've known all along it was a futile attempt. Sooner or later, people sniff out the darkness I have in me. For all that I trick and deceive, I cannot hide my true nature forever.

Back when we were teens, Daniel was the only one who got close to me without expecting my body in return, despite how he wanted me. Because of course I knew he wanted me. I noticed his lingering looks and the clench of his jaw when I looked at him. I wanted him too, but I couldn't let myself have him. Instead, I went for mean-looking guys who held me down and fucked me like they hated me, hissing slurs in my ear. Guys who'd push me into the school lockers and call me a faggot after they'd just fucked my throat.

Unlike them, Daniel was kind. But I didn't want kind; I wanted pain. So after the graduation party, I freaked the fuck out. Not only had he now proven he was just like the rest of them—by taking advantage of me when I was all but defenseless—I could not give him what he wanted. I couldn't handle his love, twisted as I was. Twisted as we had become.

It took a long time to push all those memories to the back of my mind, to suppress them all like I'm so good at doing. Every day, I wanted to come back to him, but I couldn't. Not for many years.

When I finally returned, I got it in black and white that he hated me enough to treat me the way I wanted. The fury and hurt in his eyes held all the fire I needed. No friendship, no love. Only hatred.

Hatred is the purest emotion, and when channeled into sex, it overrides everything. It takes me off and away, to a place where nothing matters but pleasure, pain, and getting pounded into oblivion.

But that's not how things turned out. Daniel had every reason to hate me for the way I hurt him and left him, but instead of hating me, he once again proved his kindness, where no one has ever been kind to me before.

It pushed me off-balance. It made me let my guard down and develop these feelings I never planned, wanted, or asked for. It's all his fault. He forced them out of me.

My eyes burn, and I shut them as my hands claw at the floor, fingers curling into tight fists.

No ... it's my fault for going after him in the first place. Or at least, it's my fault for not keeping our relationship the no-strings-attached hate-fucking it should have been.

This is what happens when you open up to someone: It might feel good for a while, but the initial relief is always followed by pain and regret.

I should have known. No one in this world can stand me for very long. Daniel had a good run at it, but when push comes to shove, I'm too fucked up for even him to handle. Too twisted and tainted by my past, by what happened in this house and the fucked-up shit I do to deal with it.

And if Daniel can't stand me, who will?

George is right about me; I'm an asshole, and there's no hope I'll ever change. It's apparent in how I treat people and in how I treat myself. I don't blame Daniel for the disgust in his face when he looked through those pictures, and I don't blame him for leaving. After all, what do I have to offer?

I have my looks, but looks fade. I have my tight ass and cock-hungry mouth. But beneath all that, there's a dark hole in me that nothing and no one can fill.

And Daniel ... Daniel deserves more than my darkness. He should be free, away from my shackles holding him down. He should find someone without a dark hole in them, someone who won't weigh him down and cling to him like a leech.

Alongside the nausea welling up my throat, tears spring to my eyes. It's not just his perfect, girthy cock that hit me in all the right places that I'm grieving. It's more than that.

It's his smile in the sunlight. It's the amused, fond tilt of his mouth, reserved only for me. It's the timbre of his voice, the strength of his arms, and the warmth of his body wrapped safely around mine.

Now I'll never experience that again.

I let out a single, heaving sob before wiping my eyes with my forearm, harsh enough to hurt. One thing's for sure: I was a lot less pathetic when I was alone and needed no one. Well, that's not exactly true, but at least I needed people for one purpose only.

It's time for me to need no one again.

I better go someplace where there're people who won't try to fix what can't be fixed. People who can shut me up and treat me like I deserve to be treated. Turn my thoughts off and reduce me to the barest, basest sense of who I am.

There's a hole in me, and someone's gotta fill it.

Chapter 16

DANIEL

Waking up at six in the morning for work feels like a blessing. To be ordered around and lift heavy things until I'm soaked in sweat is exactly what I need, to keep my body busy and my thoughts at bay.

But for some reason, work isn't as good of a distraction as it used to be. My thoughts keep straying, and I go for a run in the afternoon to clear my head. Despite my attempts to stop them, my thoughts start spinning again as my feet pummel the ground.

How the fuck am I supposed to get past this? It was hard enough when I was eighteen. With nothing but a few words, Nathan can rip my heart from my chest, throw it to the ground, and step on it with his steel-toed boots. I knew this from the start. So why the hell did I think it was a good idea to open myself up to be hurt again?

There's one difference though: This time, it was my choice to leave. That should give me at least *some* relief, but it doesn't. If anything, it makes the whole thing feel like a waste, because now Nathan is hurt too. I opened the floodgates to the most painful parts of his past, and then I left him alone to drown in it.

For all that I'm pissed at him, it wasn't fair to do what I did. But what else was I supposed to do? He hurt me. He hurt me by tagging me along in this game of his—by pretending we have something special when we don't.

George was right. Nathan cares only for himself, and he doesn't love me; he's incapable of love. All he cares about is his own needs being met, with no regard for the consequences or who he might hurt along the way.

He expected me to open up my heart to him without bothering to do the same in return. He knew damn well how capable he was of upending my life, and he didn't care—that's fucking apparent. Maybe he *does* deserve what I did. Maybe I made the right choice in leaving him to do what he does best: looking out for number one and wreaking havoc on everyone else's lives in the process.

I was an idiot for thinking I could get him to stay here and an even bigger idiot for thinking he wanted me—for *me* and not for some twisted way of dealing with his trauma. For the hundredth time, I wish he would've told me what he's been through. It would have made things easier. But at the same time, part of me wishes I could have gone on unknowing, blissfully unaware.

Now that I know what he's been through—what he's *still* putting himself through—I refuse to be a compliant piece of the puzzle. I refuse to be one of his abusers, and I refuse to accept that I might be one already because of what happened at the grad party ... Because of what I did to him ...

I run and run until I feel sick, until I feel like I'm gonna pass out. Hunched over, I grip a lamppost with both hands and yell an incoherent curse. Once I've caught my breath, I keep running. And running. And running.

Dinnertime comes and goes. By nine, there's a knock on my door.

It's April. She carries a plate of spaghetti carbonara with George on her heel.

"Hey," she says in a soft, careful voice. "You didn't come down for dinner, so we thought—"

"Have you been crying?" George asks gruffly.

"No."

"But something's gone down, right? With *him*?"

My glare probably isn't as convincing with my eyes glazed over with tears. George and April exchange a look.

"Called it," George says.

"Do you want to talk about it?" April asks.

I glance between the two of them. "I'll talk to you," I say, nodding to April. "But not to him." I don't feel like enduring his *I told you so*'s on top of everything else.

George huffs. "She's my girlfriend; she'll tell me everything anyway."

April shrugs and smiles apologetically. "He's right. But we're here for you, Daniel. Zero judgments," she adds, giving George a look.

"Yeah," he says with a nod. "Zero judgments."

"You really expect me to believe that?"

"Come on, Daniel. You're like my baby brother, you know that. I haven't seen you like this since ... you know. If it's something Nathan did, if he hurt you ... You know I won't hesitate one second to give him what he deserves. But if you just want to talk, then I'll keep calm, all right? We'll just listen if that's what you want."

I step back, inviting them into my room. "Okay."

It's not like they can fix anything anyway. Everything's already said, done, dusted, and ruined, and Nathan is probably on his way out of town as we speak.

George fiddles with a set of my drawings on my desk while April sits in the lotus position next to me on the bed.

Where do I even start? "So, uh ... Nathan and I had a fight."

"Yeah," George says. "That's pretty fucking obvious."

April glares at him, then looks back to me and speaks in a gentle tone. "What happened?"

It's not my place to tell them, but if I don't, I'll have to live with the knowledge myself, and I'm not sure I can do that. So I tell them everything I know: the photographs, Theresa, and the abuse Nathan suffered at the hands of those men. But I leave everything about the grad party unsaid.

George grimaces. "Well, shit. Poor bastard."

"That's horrible," April says, face pale.

"Do you think Wayne knew about this?" I ask with a glare directed at George, who shakes his head.

"I don't know, Daniel. If he did, he hasn't mentioned it to me. My mom found out about the stuff with Theresa, that's the only reason I know."

I smile bitterly. "Well, even if he did know, he would've incriminated himself if he told anyone."

"Again," George says, "I don't know."

"Your mom knew, yet they're still together?"

"That shit is complex, Daniel."

"You're the one who thinks Nathan is a horrible person just because he doesn't follow society's rules to a T."

"It's not just society's rules he doesn't follow. It's social cues too. Manners."

I roll my eyes. "Whatever."

"Let's get back to you and Nathan," April says. "So you found out about the photos. What happened next?"

"Well, it sort of led to us talking about graduation day." This is the bad part—the part I'd like to forget. "So basically ... We had sex at a party that night. I thought he wanted it at the time, but turns out he didn't."

"But ... he was drunk, right?" April asks.

"Yeah, like hell. We both were."

"So even if he said he wanted it, you know he couldn't consent, right?"

"I ... I know that."

"So you get what this means? You understand what you did?"

"I ..." I close my mouth. At some level, I always knew that what happened between us wasn't right, but the gravity of what I did, how badly I hurt him ... I didn't get it. The pain of him leaving me always overshadowed the guilt of my own actions, but I did worse to him than he ever did to me. I didn't understand—not until now, so long after the fact.

What I did makes me no better than his abusers. Worse—because he trusted me, and I betrayed that trust out of my own selfish needs. I chased Eric and Tyler away, yeah, but that should've been it. I should have gotten Nathan dressed and taken him out of there. But he reached for me. He kissed me, and I was so elated at having him—responsive and pliant, his hand fumbling for my fly ... I thought he wanted me, and I wanted it so badly to be true.

So I took him. I forced my own twistedness onto him when he couldn't reject it.

I hurt him.

"God. Oh god." I press the heels of my hands into my eyes and shake back and forth. Tears seep into my sweaty palms, and I can barely breathe through the tightness in my throat. "I'm ... I'm such a fucking idiot."

"You kind of are," George says. "But ... we all do stupid shit when we're drunk. Don't be too hard on yourself."

"What do I do?" I whine, the world a cold and horrible blackness behind my stinging eyes. "What the hell do I do?"

April puts a hand on my shoulder. "It's okay. You made a mistake. You were drunk, and—"

"It's not okay. Fuck, it's not okay."

Nathan needed me to protect him and care for him, but I not only failed to do so—I did the opposite. He can't forgive me for that, not when I can't even forgive myself.

"There's something I don't get," April says. "When he came back to town, the first thing he did was get in touch with you. If you hurt him, why would he have wanted that?"

"Because of convenience," I say, sniffling around a sob. "Because he needed someone to sleep with while he was here. He told me so himself."

"I'm not so sure that's the whole truth."

"Well, the alternative is worse." *That he used me to hurt himself.*

George shrugs. "Yeah, I dunno. Dude's a little fucked up." He does a loop-the-loop with his finger by his head. "Who knows how his weird little brain works? Maybe he just thought you were hot. Don't overthink it."

"I'm fucked up too. More fucked up than he is." At least Nathan only picks on people his own size. To everyone else, he's got a good heart in him. To Jessie. To animals. And to an extent, to me. Again and again, he's shown me he's not the heartless jerk he makes himself out to be at first glance. Meanwhile, I've been stuck in my own head, thinking he didn't care enough about me. As it turns out, I deserved everything he's done.

I deserved to be left and abandoned for five years. All I wish is that he would've talked to me, but at the same time, I understand why he couldn't.

Even if we find a way back to each other, how can I make sure I don't hurt him again? Maybe the only way I can have him in my life is by keeping my distance. I definitely shouldn't be having sex with him. Perhaps we can be friends, then. Distant friends. But that's not the way we are; we burn together, hot and bright. The heat we generate burns scars into him and into me. How can I help him heal when he doesn't want to? How can I soothe his burns instead of making them worse? Nathan is charred to begin with; he doesn't need any more fire to burn his flesh.

"I hurt him," I say, head hanging pitifully to my chest, "and now I can't make things right."

"Don't be so sure," April says. "Maybe you guys can still work it out. People who love each other usually do."

"Nathan doesn't love me."

April and George share a look.

"What?" I ask.

April smiles knowingly. "I don't know if you've met the guy, but he's head over heels for you."

I stare at her, jaw slack.

"Oh, come on," she says. "I've seen the way he looks at you. And the way you talk about each other ... There might be pain there, and frustration. But there's love too."

"Yeah," George says with a cough. "The dude is down bad for you, tell you that much."

"How do you know?"

"Well, he's an open book, isn't he?" April says.

"Is he?" George and I ask in unison. Nathan is a lot of things, but an open book is not one of them.

"His face is really expressive, isn't it?" Her bracelets jingle as she gestures to her own face. "He's so easy to read."

"Enlighten us," George mutters.

She leans forward, gesturing carefully with her hands. "It's obvious, isn't it? He's been hurt, and he's put walls up to prevent being hurt again. He pretends nothing affects him, and he seems strong, but underneath all that, all he really wants is to love and be loved in return."

In the corner of my vision, I see George sort of ... deflate. His crossed arms fall, and he stares at April as if he's never seen her before.

"He let you in," April continues, pointing a finger at me. "Twice, if you think about it. I suspect it's not something he's used to, and it's a gift not easily given. Right now, he probably feels like you didn't acknowledge the courage it took for him to hand you that gift."

I look down in my lap, frowning. "It took courage for me too."

"Yes, you were both very brave. But if you truly love him, you must be even braver. Nathan needs someone to accept him for who he is, flaws and all. I think, deep down, he trusted you to do that, but ..."

"But I didn't," I grit out, clenching against the tears that threaten to spill anew. "I let him down."

"It doesn't mean it's too late to fix it."

"What if he doesn't want me to?"

She smiles softly. "I think you know the answer to that question."

"Shit." Panic shoots through my veins as I remember. "He might've already left town."

"Well, in that case, what are you waiting for?" George asks. "Yeah, I said it," he mutters at my perplexed stare. "Go on. Get him back. And since you won't be finishing this ..." He grabs my forgotten dinner plate and spins a fork into the spaghetti.

"Okay," I say after a deep, determined sigh.

I'll go to him. Even if I have to chase him down on the highway, I'll beg for his forgiveness and tell him I *do* accept him, messed-up past, flaws, and all.

I can only hope he'll accept me in return.

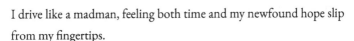

I drive like a madman, feeling both time and my newfound hope slip from my fingertips.

What if he doesn't want to see me? What if he turns me away? What if he's already left?

I won't be here waiting for you.

Oh god. He didn't mean ... did he?

Suddenly Theresa's death doesn't feel like an accident. Don't tell me he'll follow in her footsteps ... No, please no ...

The driveway is empty when I arrive. I bang on the door and call for his name. No reply. Shit, shit ... What do I do? Where is he?

I turn around with my hands raking my hair. The old neighbor with the dog is passing by the road, and I hurry over to them and yell, "Hey! Have you seen Nathan?"

"I thought I told you to keep an eye on that boy."

"I lost him, I'm sorry." I gesture to the road. "Did you see what direction he went?"

"Well, why don't you look at it like this: Where would he go if he was feeling lost?"

If he was feeling lost ... Shit, he's *there*, isn't he?

"I think I know where to find him now. Thanks."

"Don't lose him again, boy," the old man says, waving at me as I speed away.

When I arrive, Joshua and some other guy I don't recognize sit by the entrance. They both stand as I approach, and the guard dog—still leashed to the wall—starts growling and barking.

"Where is he?"

"Where's who?" Joshua drawls, a bottle of beer in one hand and a cigarette in the other.

"Who do you think? Nathan. I need to see him." I take a step closer, but Joshua and his friend block my way.

"Whoa, who said you were invited?"

"I need to talk to him."

"He looked pretty messed up when he stumbled in here, you know. What did you do to him?" Joshua takes a drag on his cigarette and blows smoke in my face. "Thought you two were an item."

"We are."

"If you were, he wouldn't have come here, would he?"

"Are you gonna let me in or not?"

"Maybe he doesn't want to see you. Maybe he's busy, doing what sluts do best."

"Move, or you'll be sorry," I growl.

His face breaks into a grin. "Hey, you found out? No wonder the guy's a little messed up in the head, am I right? Who knows what went on out in that house. Ain't no one ever seen who the baby daddy was."

My hands ball into fists. "Step. Aside." Nathan is in there, and there's no way I'll let these assholes stop me from seeing him.

Chapter 17

NATHAN

So I ENDED UP here after all. What a joke.

Half-dressed, writhing, and panting on a leather couch with a man on top of me. Part of me is someplace else, floating away with the beat of my heart, swimming in the pleasant buzz of drugs in my veins.

Wait ... who is sliding his tongue into my mouth and palming my crotch? Who does that manly, musky scent of mint, sweat, and cologne come from?

Sideburns scratch my cheek, and a jean-clad thigh parts my legs, and ... Yeah, it's him. That biker ... The bouncer from the party. The guy I tried to pick up at Moe's Den all those weeks ago. I don't remember his name, so in my mind, I call him Moe. Not that it matters what his name is. For tonight he's just my ticket to the fuck I so desperately need.

The heat of his hard body presses against mine, down onto the couch where countless others have no doubt gotten their fill before me. Girls with short skirts and smudged mascara. Guys with bared collarbones and slack, open mouths.

I groan into the kiss, but something feels off ... or maybe just different. With the cocktail of drugs in my system, I can't really tell.

This used to feel right. It used to feel like the only correct thing in my sad excuse for a life. But it doesn't feel the same as it once did. Don't tell me Daniel ruined casual sex for me too. It's all I have left.

"Hey!" someone yells from outside, followed by the dull thud of a body hitting a wall. "All right, all right! But make it quick."

I break the kiss and put my hands on Moe's chest. "What's going on?"

"Don't worry about them," he says, leaning in to kiss me again.

A door slams open, and footsteps barge into the room. Next thing I know, someone rips Moe away from me, and he doubles over from a punch to the gut.

Daniel looms behind him, a thunderous expression on his face. "Get out."

"Dude, what the fuck," Moe growls and grabs him by the shirt, fist raised.

"Go ahead," Daniel says, nostrils flaring.

They glare at each other for a few moments. With a snort and a "fuck this," Moe stumbles out of the room.

As soon as we're alone, Daniel shifts his attention to me. "Get up."

"Here to finish the job?" I ask, spreading my legs to clarify the meaning.

"No. I'm taking you home." His hand reaches out for me, and his knuckles ... His knuckles are tinged with red.

"Oh, baby," I drawl, "is that blood?"

I haven't seen Daniel fight in ... how long? He should show this side of himself more often; he's hot when he's angry.

"I said, get up." Sick of waiting for me to take his hand, he grabs my upper arm and pulls me to my feet.

I struggle against his hold. "Lemme go."

"What did you take?"

"Not sure. A bit of this, a bit of that. Feels good, though, and I was about to feel even better. If you're not gonna finish what he started, you might as well leave."

"I'm not going to leave you. You're coming with me."

I lean backward, but instead of hitting the couch, I sway unsteadily, and Daniel catches me by the shoulder. I feel faint—untethered to my own limbs and estranged from my mind. Then again, I don't remember the last proper meal I got in me. It might be that. Might also be the insane amounts of alcohol and drugs I've consumed these past few days.

"What if I don't want to?" Again, I try to shake him off. My childish stubbornness drives even *me* mad sometimes, but now I want to ride that wave. Daniel deserves to sweat a bit. "Come on." I grab onto him and slide my arms around his neck. "Just continue where the other guy left off. I know you want to." *Prove to me you're just like them so I can stop caring about you, because caring about you hurts.*

"I thought you agreed to quit fucking other people."

"Well yeah, but that was before you broke things off with me and left me alone in that house!"

His eyes soften. "I'm sorry about that."

"Whatever." I glare at him, delighting in the uncertainty that flickers across his face.

"I want to talk to you," he says and glances around the room—at the empty beer cans, the drug paraphernalia, and the general filthy state of the place. "But not here."

"Why not? Whatever you want to say to me, you can say it right here."

His face twists with frustration. "Could you at least put your shirt on?"

"It's nothing you haven't seen before, baby," I say with a smirk and an obscene gesture with my hips. "Or does it distract you too much? Won't be able to help yourself?"

He throws my shirt at me. "Just shut up and put it on."

I do as he says. Not sober enough for rational thinking, I suppose. I feel out of sorts, and not just because of the drugs and the vodka.

"So ... you hate me now, right?" I look up at him, biting my lip in a sideways pout. "I'm an asshole, and you can't stand the sight of me. Is that what you came here to say?"

"No."

"That's what you told me. You said it would be best if I leave again."

His chest heaves in a sad excuse for a laugh. "I don't hate you, Nathan. Don't you get it?"

"Get what?" Mouth set in a hard line, I cross my arms over my chest.

He looks annoyed and resigned at the same time. His face scrunches up as if he's in pain, though he smiles through it.

"I love you."

The words ring in my ears, but they don't stick. Are the booze and drugs playing tricks on me, spinning lies I'm too far gone to understand?

"You what?" My lower lip trembles. I feel like crying.

"Do you want me to say it again?"

"Yes." It comes out a whisper—a raw, pathetic one.

"I love you. I love you, Nathan," he says, and his hand brushes my cheek. "I always have."

Holy shit. Holy shit. My heart beats as if it's trying to break through my ribs.

"Even when I'm being a jerk to you? Or to your friends?"

"Yes," he says, voice firm. "I feel it constantly, all the time. Even when I try to hate you, I always end up loving you in the end."

I close my eyes, and for now, I allow myself to believe. I beg the universe to *please let it be true*. I've been in the dark for so long, oh please let me have this one thing ... This one beam of light in my life.

But ... "What about that stuff?"

"What stuff?"

"The pictures. The stuff you saw."

The stuff I've told no one except for him.

The stuff I should've taken with me to the grave.

That's what started this whole thing, isn't it? Daniel couldn't handle how damaged I am. He freaked out. He deemed me unsalvageable, unfixable, just like everyone would if they knew what he does now.

"Oh, Nathan," he says, voice pained. "It wasn't your fault. None of it."

Usually I can't stand pity, because there's no way anyone can understand all the shit I've been through, and I don't *want* them to understand. But with Daniel, it feels less like he's pretending to understand and more like he's just sad and angry on my behalf.

Maybe that's what makes the words spill from my mouth.

"I've tried to get rid of it, all right? I've tried to control it—all this ... all this *badness* in me." I clutch my chest, and tears well up in my eyes. "But I can't. What if I'm broken and can't be fixed? That's what she said. My mom. That I was bad and that I always would be. And those men, those pictures ... That's not all. You remember when Wayne Hastings caught us shoplifting?"

"Yeah?"

"Remember how he kept me at the station for ages? He gave me nothing to eat or drink for hours, wouldn't even let me piss. He said bad kids like me weren't meant to roam the streets and threatened to lock me up in juvie for years ... Unless I did something for him."

"Did what?"

My scoff comes out as more of a sob. "Fuck, you're clueless some-times. He made me suck his dick, okay?"

"Oh god ..."

"Yeah, that's right. The world isn't just sunshine and rainbows. But of course, I already knew that when I knelt with my hands cuffed behind my back, getting ready to suck your uncle's—"

"Stop." His hands tighten on me, his breathing rough and fast. "I'm gonna kill him. I'm gonna kill all of them."

"You get it now? You get how fucked up I am?"

"It's not you, Nate. It's *them*. They're the ones who did this to you. You were just a kid. You're not the one to blame; they are."

Goddamn it. My eyes burn, and stinging tears trickle out when I blink.

"Come here." Daniel opens his arms, and I fall into his embrace. "I've got you."

I cry into his shoulder, clutching onto him like a lifeline. "I'm sorry," I choke out, my whole body racking with a sob. "I'm sorry for leaving you. Sorry for the shit I said. Sorry for everything."

"It's okay."

"It's not."

"This kind of makes up for it."

Me crying in his arms like a blubbering mess makes up for five years of heartbreak and sorrow? That makes zero fucking sense, but okay.

"I'm sorry," I repeat and hug him closer. It's all I can say, and it's all I can do, as he strokes the back of my head and clutches me with all the strength in him, everything he means to me, and the forgiveness I thought I would never deserve.

I draw in a breath and let it out with a slump of my shoulders. "I'm tired."

"Me too. Come, I'll take you home."

Home. I wince at the image that floats into my head. Compared to the safety of Daniel's arms, the house at Wayward Road feels like something out of a horror movie. I knew from the start it wasn't good for me to live there, but I didn't care. I craved it. I wanted that horror—those memories—to sink into my chest and slice me open. But now ...

"I don't want to go back there," I say, rubbing my cheek into Daniel's chest.

"I know. You don't have to."

"I do though. I don't have anywhere else to go." I sniffle around a final, chest-heaving sob.

"We'll go to my place."

"What about George? He hates me. He'll beat the shit out of me."

"He won't. We'll spend the night there, at least. After that, we'll figure things out."

Figure things out. He makes it sound so easy, but nothing's ever easy with me—surely he must know that by now?

"B-Because ..." The words get stuck in my throat. I've never felt more pathetic than this, but Daniel doesn't seem to mind. I told him once that he likes my bite, but maybe he likes this side of me better. That would serve me right, wouldn't it? All this time, I've kept these emotions walled off, but all it took was a couple of weeks in his presence for what's been trapped in me for so long to come bursting out. It hurts, but there's relief in it too. Thousands of miles and countless hookups and orgasms couldn't do what Daniel just did. "Because you ..."

"Yeah, that's right—because I love you." He wipes my cheeks with his thumbs and smiles, despite my sobs. Because he knows my tears are not solely from pain. He *knows* me, like nobody else does. He's seen me at my darkest moments, and even after everything we've been through—even after all my fuckups and mistakes—he's still here.

He came for me. He loves me.

And when his hand reaches for mine, I take it.

Heat spreads from the arm wrapped around my waist and sunlight shines into my eyes. I turn around, and instead I face a different kind of light.

Daniel's sleep-tousled hair spreads over the pillow. His freckles and golden eyelashes seem to shimmer in the sunlight. Eyes closed softly in sleep, with the slightest wrinkle between his brows ... He's so beautiful.

My lips stretch into a hopelessly happy smile with the memory of last night. Now that I'm sober, yesterday's confession feels distant and jumbled up in my mind. I remember crying a whole lot. My face feels puffy and my eyes sore and dry. I remember us hugging. I remember him telling me that ... that he loves me.

Heat rises to my cheeks. Sure, I can joke about it, especially to tick George off. But to hear it from his own mouth and as sincerely as last night ... That's different.

No one has ever loved me. Not my grandfather, not my mom. People can love me for a short while, sure, like when I'm cracking a spot-on joke or when they're balls-deep inside of me.

But I know that's not what Daniel meant. He wouldn't use that tone of voice if he weren't sincere. Daniel's not like me; he wouldn't lie, and he doesn't play games. Right?

At least he didn't say it just so he could get me home and fuck me; otherwise, he would've done it already, and as muddled as my memory is, I don't remember us having sex last night. All he did was help me out of my clothes, put me to bed, and wrap me in his strong embrace.

He brought me here to take care of me. To let me sleep off my days-long bender. Speaking of a hangover: Despite my wickedly dry mouth and my pounding head, I don't feel all that bad. I do feel hungry though. My gut is like a black hole, ready to swallow just about anything.

I sit up from the bed, but before my feet land on the floor, a hand grabs my arm and pulls me back.

"How are you feeling?" Daniel asks.

"Starving. And thirsty as hell."

He hands me a bottle of water. "Here."

I chug a couple of mouthfuls and glance at him, unable to hide the suspicion on my face.

"Now that you're sober," he says, "we need to talk."

There it is.

"Talk? We talked forever last night, didn't we?"

"Yeah, but not about this." He sits up and gestures for me to sit next to him. "Not about the grad party."

My face goes blank save for a slow, sarcastic tilt to my mouth. Here it goes—my final line of defense. My last-ditch attempt at keeping him away. "What's there to talk about? You had a good time, didn't you?"

He shakes his head, a pained crease between his brows. "You needed me to take care of you and take you away from that place, but I didn't save you that night. I wasn't any better than Eric and Tyler. I hurt you, and I didn't understand, and I'm sorry. I'm so sorry."

I shrug, glancing to the side. "It's fine though. I'm over it."

"Clearly you're not, and even if you were, it's not fine." He grabs my hands and envelops them with his own. "I'm so sorry, Nathan. I'm sorry I let you down. I wish I could do it over. I wish I could turn back time and know then what I do now, but I can't."

"You didn't let me down."

"I did. Please tell me I did. If I didn't, it just means you didn't expect better from me."

"It's not that simple."

He smiles a bitter smile. "Well, at least one thing became simple after that night: You didn't feel the same for me as I felt for you. I was in love with you, and you treated me like I was dirt. We were supposed to be friends, and I ruined it—I know I did. But you hurt me too. You gotta know you hurt me too."

"I've already told you; I *do* know that, and I'm sorry, okay? And that other stuff is fine, I—"

"It's not fine. And you leaving me for five years proves you didn't think it was fine either."

My lower lip trembles. Why? Why do I feel like crying all of a sudden? I wept enough last night. I wept enough for a lifetime.

"Tell me I hurt you," Daniel says.

I nod, afraid I'll break into tears if I talk.

"Say it."

"You hurt me," I whisper, swallowing against the thickness in my throat.

"And nothing I say can ever make it right. That's why I'm giving you a choice."

"A choice?" My pulse quickens. I don't like the sound of this, not at all.

"I can't stand it if you're hurting yourself by being with me. Maybe we can't be together in a healthy way. Maybe it's better if we're apart."

"What?" I rip my hands away from him and shoot to my feet. "Fuck no! Look." I point between us. "You're my best friend. You're the only one who's ever even *liked* me. You think I'd throw that away just because you did what all guys do when they have me naked in bed?"

"I wanted to be different from them. I ruined it."

"Maybe you did, but fuck, Daniel, what's done is done! You were drunk, same as me, and I hurt you too. We hurt each other. I won't let you throw me out just because of your messed-up guilt and savior complex, okay? I've been with men who hurt me, who hurt me badly, and I know the difference. You're not them. You're good to me. You're the only good thing in my life. If you make me leave you, you'll hurt me more than those sadistic motherfuckers ever did. I'm lost without you. There's nothing out there for me. Only you. Don't you dare take that away from me."

He hesitates.

"Okay?" I say sternly.

"Okay," he replies.

I get dressed and walk downstairs, but when I reach the kitchen doorway, I stop dead in my tracks. It's not April who's making breakfast, as I hoped and expected.

It's George. In baggy gray sweatpants and a T-shirt, he's flipping eggs by the stove.

He glances at me over his shoulder. "Oh, you're up. Where's Daniel?"

I plop myself onto the kitchen counter next to him. "Shower."

Without a word, George prepares a plate of toast with sliced tomatoes, ham, and fried eggs. It smells fucking incredible. I bet the excitement shows on my face when he hands it to me.

"Here. You're skin and bones. Daniel not feeding you enough?"

I smirk and raise my brows. "Oh, he feeds me plenty."

George sends me a look. "Don't start."

He prepares his own plate and sits down by the kitchen table. I stay on the counter, swinging my legs and pulling my toast apart as I eat, sprinkling crumbs all over myself and the floor.

"So." George chews his last piece of toast and brushes his hands together. "I'll allow you to move in for now, just until you and Daniel find another place."

"I don't need any charity."

"Oh, this isn't charity; you'll pay for it."

"But I won't even take up any space! I'll just sleep in Daniel's room." I pick a slice of ham off the toast and dangle it into my mouth. "You won't even know I'm here."

George chuckles. "I highly doubt that."

The rest of the meal passes in silence, with George reading the news on his phone and me sipping OJ. He doesn't even look up when I start picking crumbs off my plate, rolling them between my fingers and flicking them to the floor.

Well, then. This isn't nearly as awkward as I thought it would be. It's not like I'll stick around here forever though.

I push myself to my feet and saunter into the hallway.

"Going out?" George asks.

"Just for a smoke."

"Take this, it's freezing outside." He hands me a thick woolen coat with intricate stitched patterns. Looks like something a grandma would wear, but I refrain from making the comment.

As I get outside and inhale the frigid morning air, I wonder at my hesitation to quip back at George. It's not as if I've suddenly started to like the guy. He's still the same asshole he's always been, with the same asshole father. I want this thing with Daniel to work out, though, and

I suppose that overrides my desire to piss off George. Not that I'll be some angel about it. On the other hand, when am I ever?

I lean against the porch railing and gaze out at the frost-covered lawn. A windless chill clings to the air, signaling winter's arrival.

"There you are."

I turn around. I didn't even notice the door opening.

Daniel smiles, hands in his pockets. His hair is wet, and a shadow of worry from earlier this morning still lines his face. He walks over to me and lifts his hand, brushing his finger over my lower lip.

I freeze in place. What the hell's up with me? Daniel's touched me like this loads of times; I should be used to it by now.

"Did you have breakfast?" he asks, and I nod. He adjusts the lapels of my patterned woolen coat with a smirk. "Cute jacket."

"George has shit fashion sense."

"I think this was his grandma's old coat actually. I bet you can keep it if you want."

"Whatever," I say with an eye roll, but I can't help but smile.

This is where we met—on this porch, in that crazy thunderstorm all those weeks ago. Instead of slamming me to the wall and yelling in my face like he did back then, Daniel presses me softly against the railing, hands on my hips.

I breathe through the increasing beat of my heart. "He said he'd let me stay here."

"George did?"

"Yeah. Just until you and I get a place of our own."

"So you're selling your mom's house?"

I give a one-shouldered shrug. "Well, it's either that or torch the place."

He brushes my bangs out of my face. Tugs at the hair on my nape. My eyelids flutter closed with the treatment. I feel like a dog being petted. Feels nice. Warm and safe.

This seems so easy. Maybe Daniel's right: Maybe we *will* figure this out after all. Maybe the universe will grant me this one wish. I pray I won't fuck it up this time.

He glances down to my mouth, but before his lips touch mine, I pull back a bit.

"Don't go all sappy on me now. I still want you to fuck my brains out, you know."

His smile turns sly. "Don't worry. I will." He noses into my neck, breath hot against my ear. "But I want to make love to you too."

I grimace. "Make love to me? Sounds—"

"Don't say it sounds boring," he warns.

I glance down, trying but failing to hide my blush. "Why would you want to do that?"

"Because I love you," he says plainly. "Is it really that hard to believe?"

"No. I mean, I've never ... done this before." I gesture between the two of us. "All I ever wanted from guys was to get fucked, quick and dirty. And that's all they ever wanted from me too."

Daniel cups my chin, tilting my face up to make me meet his eyes. "Want to know what I think? I think you need more than that. You need someone who'll take care of you and care for you. I'll do it. If you'll let me."

"I don't need ...," I begin, but Daniel sends me a pointed look that makes me lose all train of thought. I whisper, "Okay."

And it's like a great weight lifts from my shoulders—immense from years past, through pain and through shadow. Whenever I'm vulnerable like this, the initial relief is usually followed by pain and, with it, a childlike urge to curl in on myself. To take back what I just lost.

The relief comes first: in the warmth that fills my chest as Daniel's arms wrap around me and his hand rubs little circles at the back of my head.

I wait for the pain, but ...

It never comes.

Epilogue

DANIEL

Two months later

NATHAN LOUNGES ON THE bed, freshly showered and dressed only in a pair of tight red boxers. He watches me with an intent expression on his face: brows furrowed, mouth slightly parted. Now and again, he looks away, only for his gaze to flit back to me just as quick.

After a good ten minutes of this, I drop my pen and lean back in the chair. "Go ahead—speak your mind." So much for his promise to help with my reapplication to art school; I won't get anything done with him looking at me like that.

"I just like watching you draw, okay?" A flush creeps up his throat, and he looks away. "It's kinda ... peaceful or whatever."

I raise an eyebrow, trying to decipher what he's really trying to tell me. He's rarely this quiet, and when he is, it's because he wants to tell me something but doesn't know how.

It can't be ... *that* ... can it?

Two months after that cold, bright morning on the porch, he still hasn't told me those magic three words, even though I've told *him* more times than I can count. I've been patient with it; what he doesn't say in words, he shows me in action. But still ... Nathan can say the most heinous, fucked-up shit, but "I love you" is too much?

He does love me, though, I'm fairly sure. Almost as sure as I am about my love for him. That's not to say he doesn't drive me to the end point of my sanity sometimes, like when he steals George's protein shakes even though he obviously hates them and does it only to piss him off, or like right now, when he refuses to say what's on his mind.

I just wish he would tell me how he feels. Unprompted, like I do.

There's a knock on the door, and George sticks his head in. "Oh, come on. You guys still haven't packed up?"

"I thought you said ten."

"It *is* ten!" His gaze shifts from me to Nathan's half-naked form, and Nathan meets his eyes with a challenging half smirk.

Somehow, they've made it two months of living in the same place without killing each other. No broken noses either. Not to say there haven't been some rough times, but in a few hours, none of it will matter.

Nathan and I are moving out. It took us a while to find a one-bedroom apartment with decent rent and a good location. Took Nathan a while to get a job too, but now he works part-time at the animal shelter up north. He comes home with a tired smile on his lips, smelling of wet fur and dog treats.

By referring to Jessie's love of animals more than her love for Nathan, I convinced my mom to let me take her to the shelter once a week. Her and Nathan's encouraging coos as they feed the smallest, weakest little beagle together warm my heart more than anything else.

"I'll go get the trailer now," George says. "When I come back, I want all this shit downstairs." He waves a hand at the moving boxes and furniture.

When the door shuts, I stand up and stretch my arms over my head. "You heard him. We should be getting ready."

Nathan gazes at me from under his bangs, lips tilted in a sultry way only he can manage. I know what that look means.

"It's at least a fifteen-minute drive," he says in an innocent tone.

I give him a look. *The* look. The *are you serious right now?* look I give him at least once a day. The *quit it or I'll spank you so hard you won't be able to sit for a week* look.

"Oh, come on." He pouts. "Can I suck you off at least?"

"I don't know. Can you?" More often than not when he's in this mood, he'll end up begging me to fuck him before I come.

"Let's put it like this, what's gonna get you off faster: my mouth or my ass?"

I smile and shake my head. "There's not enough time." Despite my words, I find myself with one knee on the mattress, sliding my fingers into his hair.

He gazes up at me with an expression he knows all too well I'm hopeless to resist. "Wanna bet?"

We'll figure things out.

That's what I promised him we'd do. And that's what we're still doing.

Even though he tells me it's all good—that he likes everything I do to him, and that I'm not causing him harm—I sometimes struggle to believe it. He's lied to me before. It's so ingrained in him to neglect his own well-being that it'll take time, and a lot of coaxing on my part—and on the part of his new therapist—to mend what's been broken in him.

Some nights, he still wakes up in a cold sweat. I hold him tight while he tells me the fragments of his nightmare until his heartbeat slows back down and we can both drift back to sleep.

No, we've hardly got it all figured out. But that desperate pinch in my chest isn't there anymore. Now that all secrets are out between us—now that I know what he's dealing with—I know I can help him through it. When my confidence wanes, he pulls me back up. When his bad feelings and memories flood him, I'm there to pull him back to shore.

I cannot take away the past—neither his nor ours—but I can promise to be there for him. For us. And part of being there for him means satisfying his never-ending appetite for sex.

That's why I end up with his lips wrapped around my cock. When I rock my hips forward, he takes me all the way down his throat with ease, looking up at me with flushed cheeks and half-lidded eyes.

"We could stay like this forever, huh?" I slide my fingers into the smooth locks of his hair. "You'll never get enough of this." Neither will I. Won't ever get enough of how he shudders with relief as my cock slides into his mouth. He needs this from me, so badly. And I'm more than happy to give it to him.

He replaces his mouth with his hand and jerks me with slow, sloppy movements, licking his spit-slick lips. "Put it in. Just the tip. I know you wanna come in me."

"Fine. Get on the bed. On your stomach."

He grins and does as I tell him, tugging his boxers down and leaving them by his knees. I lube myself up in record time and push into the tight, willing heat of his body.

It never fails to amaze me how pliant he can be with my cock buried in his ass and my hand over his mouth. For all his confidence and stubbornness, in bed, he's reduced to a begging, writhing mess.

He likes it when I fuck him hard and ruthless like this, sure, but what really gets to him is when we're face-to-face. When I'm kissing him, rolling into him languidly with no hurry in the world, whispering how good he is. Yeah, that drives him properly insane. He acts like it's a punishment—as if he can't stand it—but when he comes, he throws his head back and gasps as if he's been drowning, pleasure evident in the furrow of his brow and his sweet, parted mouth.

He can claim all he wants that he doesn't like when I'm tender with him. I know the truth.

But today, I'm far from tender; I'm straight to the point, chasing my orgasm until I feel it cresting with every thrust of my hips. He gasps and writhes as I bury myself to the hilt. I'm almost there, right on the edge ... when George's voice calls on the other side of the door.

"Hey! I thought I told you two to get ready."

I snap my hips once, twice, keeping my grunts as quiet as I can while I ride through my orgasm. I gather my breath enough to yell back, "Uh, yeah! We're almost done."

Nathan glares at me over his shoulder. "I was just about to come. He ruined it."

"Told you we wouldn't have enough time. Come on. We don't wanna give George an aneurysm."

Nathan wipes his sweaty bangs out of his face and mutters, "Don't we?"

Apart from the smug smile he sends George as he exits our room, Nathan behaves surprisingly well. The move takes most of the afternoon regardless, and when we're done, the sun is already setting.

A layer of snow covers the ground of the small apartment parking lot where we say our goodbyes.

"Tell me if you need anything," April says and hugs Nathan for a long, long time. "Anything at all."

"Okay," Nathan whispers, smiling into the embrace.

My heart swells with a strange sort of pride at his newfound ability to accept help without any of his usual sarcastic remarks.

George clears his throat. "It's not like you guys are moving more than ten minutes away."

I take his outstretched hand and pull him into a hug. "Thank you." *Thank you for letting him stay. Thank you for accepting him.*

George gives a little chuckle. "I never thought I'd say this, but he's not that bad. You really mellow him out."

"Don't say that to his face. He'll take it as a challenge."

Nathan turns to us, viper quick. "Don't say what to my face?"

"Nothing."

April gives me a long, tight hug, and soon after that, Nathan and I are left alone to our new home.

The apartment has an open floor plan with a bathroom to the right and a small bedroom by the balcony door. It's not much, but it's ours. I can't wait to fall asleep every night with him in my arms and wake up every morning to his sleep-tousled hair and the shy, happy smile that nowadays isn't as rare as it used to be.

"Come here."

Nathan hops off the kitchen counter he plopped himself onto. His arms sling around my shoulders, body pressed tight against mine.

"It's kind of cold in here," he says.

"I'll keep you warm."

He hums and clutches me closer. "We'll keep warm together."

It's such a simple thing, but coming from Nathan, it means the world. A great possessive urge sweeps through me as my arms tighten around his waist. Mine. He's mine. Only I get to have him.

He's been roughed up and abused in every which way—more ways than I can probably imagine. Life has held him under, but I'll lift him up. He's mine to hold, mine to fuck, mine to protect. And I'm his.

"Fuck, I love you so much," I mumble into the crook of his neck.

There's a hitch of breath, and a muffled, "Me too," against my shoulder.

I pull back. "What?"

"I said, me too."

"Yeah, but tell me what you mean by that."

He frowns, and his mouth opens and closes. "Just that I … love you too is all."

My chest swells with warmth. *Finally.* Finally he said it. It's not like I didn't know, but to hear it confirmed feels even better than I thought it would. Still, I can't help but tease him.

"That's all? Way to downplay it."

He scowls, cheeks flushing pink. "Shut up."

I kiss him—first his pretty, plump mouth, then his jaw, then his throat. "Say it again." I slide my hand down his back and into the hem of his jeans.

"I love you." His fingers tangle into my hair, and he lets out a hopelessly breathy groan as my finger slips into his crack, prodding and pressing his tight, willing hole. "Oh *fuck*. I love you. I love you."

He shudders into my embrace, and I lick away the salty tears that trickle down his cheek. I root myself in him, and he roots himself in me.

We'll take care of each other. We'll make a home together and make a home in each other. My best friend. My ride-or-die. My Nathan. His tears are mine to dry, his holes are mine to fill, and not a day goes by that I don't bask in the impossibility of this new, hard-fought truth.

THE END

Afterword

Sign up to my newsletter to access a **bonus chapter**! Go to allyavery author.com/subscribe.

Dear Reader,

Thank you so much for giving my debut novel *Getting It Twisted* a chance!

The characters in this book are flawed and make mistakes, and sometimes their reality isn't pretty or ideal. I've always found a happy ending more impactful if the main characters have gone through hell to get it. Please keep in mind there are a lot of ways trauma and PTSD can affect a person, and Nathan's experience is just one of them.

If you found a typo that snuck past numerous rounds of editing, feel free to send me an email at **contact@allyaveryauthor.com** and let me know.

Reviews are invaluable to indie authors like myself and help us reach more readers, so please consider leaving a review for *Getting It Twisted* on Amazon and/or Goodreads.

Thank you so much for reading. I hope we meet again!

Ally

Also by Ally Avery

Breaking You Open

In the second book in the Unforgivable Needs series, *Breaking You Open*, a young college student on the run from his abusive ex finds unlikely refuge in a gruff older biker haunted by a violent past.

Blurb

Sparrow

He's the one I need.

When a smoking hot older biker saves me from a miserable night, I know I can call him home. But my dream soon turns into a nightmare when he kicks me out.

Next thing I know, the past I've fought to escape comes back to haunt me. But I know where I can take refuge.

If he'll have me.

Louis

I'm not the one he needs.

And he's not mine to take.

Too young. Too frail. Too broken.

But he insists he needs me, and who am I to refuse when a cute boy with pouty lips and haunted eyes shows up on my doorstep?

His demons are hot on his heels, and he counts on me for protection. But how can I protect him, if I can't even protect him from myself?

Get it on Amazon

About the author

Ally found her love for reading and writing at a young age. MM romance in particular has been part of her life since her first exposure to late-2000s Shounen Ai.

She likes to write about fierce, damaged boys who need a lot of love, and she doesn't shy away from dark and taboo topics that some readers might find disturbing. *Getting It Twisted* is her debut novel.

You can follow her on Instagram (@authorallyavery) and Facebook, and check out her website allyaveryauthor.com for updates on upcoming projects, releases, and more.

Made in United States
Troutdale, OR
03/30/2025

30177764R00136